Fc of Fire and Ice

A Paranormal Dating Agency Story

One is good, two is better!
Roxanne Witherell

By: Roxanne Witherell

For the Love of Fire and Ice
Paranormal Dating Agency
Copyright 2018 Roxanne Witherell
Published by MT Worlds Press, Inc.
Winter Springs, FL 32708
http://mtworldspress.com
Cover art by: Glowing Moon Cover Designs
Edited by: Liz Wilks
Formatting by Celtic Formatting

All rights reserved under the International and Pan-American Copyright Conventions. No part of this book may be reproduced or transmitted in any form or by any means, electronic or mechanical, including photocopying, recording, or by any information storage and retrieval system, without permission in writing from the publisher.

This is a work of fiction. Names, places, characters and incidents are either the product of the author's imagination or are used fictitiously, and any resemblance to any actual persons, living or dead, organizations, events or locales, is entirely coincidental.

http://mtworldspress.com

Dedication

For my wonderful sister, Heather, who's always there pushing me further into my potential. For all the wonderful readers out there, you keep me going. I want to thank each one of you for your support. This is truly a wonderful adventure that wouldn't be possible without readers to share my stories with. There's so much more to share with you.

Acknowledgement

I want to send out a special thanks to Milly Taiden for creating the wonderful world of Paranormal Dating Agency. I look forward to writing many more books in the PDA world.

One

Annette watched as newlyweds, Ronan and Braelynn, made their way to the front of the room. Annette knew her best friend had finally found her happiness. One day, she'd find that kind of happiness of her own. Until then, she'd continue to surf on the ocean of men. Plucking one out every now and then. She just hadn't found a man she'd actually commit to.

Ronan pulled Braelynn's garter off with his teeth and flicked it behind him into the group of single men. His best man, Greyson, caught the garter and cheers erupted. Knowing the bouquet toss would be next, Annette made her way toward the center of the room. Suddenly, she was bumped from the side causing her to lose balance for a moment.

"Sorry," Annette said grabbing on to the closest arm beside her.

"No worries. Everyone gets in an uproar at this part of a wedding reception." The top of the woman's head was just over Annette's shoulder.

"I wasn't," Annette began but was caught in the rush of single women heading to the center.

Looking back, Annette searched for the woman. Short white hair caught Annette's eyes as the woman weaved through the crowd of onlookers. The woman seemed familiar. She racked her brain as she made her way to the front of the group, where Braelynn told her to stand. The woman smiled at her. With a nod Annette hoped to convey her apology for being rude and rushing off.

"Alright ladies. It's that time." Ronan called out and more women joined the group.

Crossing her fingers, Annette hoped she wasn't going to have to fight anyone over the bouquet. Braelynn glanced at her then turned back around, tossing the bouquet into the air. Instead of soaring to the center of the crowd, it hit the ceiling beam causing it to drop straight down to Annette. She jumped up stretching out her arm. She grabbed hold of the bouquet just as two more sets of hands came her way. They missed their mark. A few mumbled curses and some congratulations, then the crowd dispersed.

"Great catch," the woman said walking up to her. "I'm Gerri Wilder."

"You're the one that hooked Braelynn up with Ronan. I thought I recognized you," she said.

"That's right. I could do the same for you, too," Gerri offered.

Looking at Braelynn and Ronan, she watched as they shared a few kisses while dancing. Remembering the way Braelynn described flying with Ronan geared her into a decision.

"I'll take one like Ronan. Hell, I'll take two," she claimed with a smiled.

"Be careful what you wish for," Gerri warned her.

"I wish for two sexy men to sweep me off my feet." Of course, she didn't really expect two men, but the thought of being with two had always turned her on.

For the next half hour, she sat with Gerri talking like they hadn't seen each other in years. Gerri asked a bunch of random questions. At least they seemed random to her but Gerri assured her it was to help find the perfect match. Gerri gave her a hug before she left the party. Annette spotted BJ sitting alone, and decided to keep her company.

"You two seemed cozy," BJ stated, nodding towards Gerri as she left.

"Does this mean you changed your mind?" Braelynn came over to the table.

"It means I'll give it a try." She looked up at Braelynn, who was grinning from ear to ear.

"You're going to be glad you did. I'm telling you, that woman can work magic on your love life."

"My love life is fine. It's finding someone I don't want to strangle after a week that's the problem."

"That's still your love life." Braelynn laughed.

"Fine! Yes, my love life could use a little help then," she admitted. Jules came to the table with a plate of cake, and sat down beside her.

"What'd I miss?" Jules said forking a piece of cake in her mouth.

"Annette's struggling love life." BJ laughed.

"Hey," Annette stuck her tongue out at BJ. "It's not that bad."

"How many men have you gone through in the last six months?" Braelynn asked, putting her hand on her hip.

"Not as many as you, but that's beside the point."

"Sounds like that is the point." Jules pointed her fork at Annette.

"I can't help it. Guys are aggravating. Here lately, they're all selfish ass nuggets. It's always how I can please them. Then get mad when I call them out on it," she explained.

"You can't be hot and cold. Guys don't know what to do with women like that. I bet whoever Gerri finds will be perfect," Braelynn said, twisting in her seat. "I mean, look who she found for me."

"Thinking of me, beautiful." Ronan came over with his hands loaded with wine glasses. "Ladies," he offered each of them a glass.

"I'm always thinking of you," Braelynn smiled up at him. "Everything will be fine," she assured Annette as Ronan bent down to kiss his wife.

"We'll see." Annette hoped to hear from Gerri soon. She followed BJ and Jules onto the dance floor, leaving Braelynn and Ronan to their newly wedded bliss.

Two

"I still think we could have gone to the wedding," Bryan said, walking over to Tony.

"We need to get the twelfth floor open so we can start on the basement level before summer starts," Tony informed him for the tenth time.

"We'll get it done. One evening of fun would have been nice. Plus, all Braelynn's girlfriends were there. We'd finally get to meet them."

"If Braelynn couldn't get those women to come into our regular club, what makes you think they would be okay with us? Heads N' Tails is who we are. They'd have to accept us and this whole establishment."

"It's possible for us to find a woman that will." Bryan leaned against the kitchen counter and pulled Tony into his arms. "Ronan said he called

Gerri at Paranormal Dating Agency. Maybe we should too. It's not like we leave this building much."

"We have everything we need here. Besides, we don't need a dating agency," Tony insisted.

"Tony, you work every floor here. No one has pushed the right buttons for us. Casual women don't count. We need to branch out."

"Aren't I enough for you?" Tony grabbed Bryan's shirt, pulling it over his head.

"Of course, you are. But you know as well as I do, that's only half of who we are. We need our other half, our female. She's out there, somewhere." Bryan pulled Tony's shirt off, exposing his muscular chest. "How about some fun before we go into work tonight?"

"I was wondering if you were taking my hint." Tony smiled, and pressed his lips to Bryan's. "Whoever gets there first gets to bat."

Tony took off toward the bedroom, but Bryan wasn't worried. With longer legs, he was able to get in front of Tony. Once he was in the bedroom he jumped on the bed, taking his claim.

"I let you win tonight," Tony stated, pulling off his jeans and leaving them on the floor.

"Sure you did." Bryan wiggled out of his pants and dropped them off the side of the bed. "Why don't you park that sweet cock over here? I'll reward you for your efforts." He patted the spot beside him.

"Hell yeah!" Tony crawled into bed, turned around, and laid with his feet near the headboard.

Tony's cock was perfectly positioned in front of Bryan. With only an hour before they had to be back downstairs, Bryan didn't waste any time. Firmly gripping Tony's cock, Bryan pumped it a couple of times as he leaned in taking him into his mouth. After years together, Bryan knew exactly how Tony wanted it. Just as Tony knew how he liked it. Tony's gentle caresses and soft lips stroked Bryan's hard cock. Pleasure built inside him, and he tightened his grip on Tony's cock. Not wanting to come right now, Bryan got up. While Tony laid on his back, Bryan grabbed the bottle of lube from the nightstand. He applied some to the head of his cock and put the bottle back. Tony smiled up at him while scooting over, laying on his back. Bryan positioned himself between Tony's legs, spreading Tony's ass checks for a smoother thrust.

"Go deep," Tony said, as Bryan pushed inside of him.

Bryan thrust deep as he took Tony's cock in his hands, pumping to the same rhythm. Tony reached up pinching Bryan's nipples, and flicked his nipple ring.

"Wouldn't you like a nice tight pussy wrapped around your cock as I thrust into you?" Bryan squeezed Tony's cock as he pumped.

"Yeah," Tony breathed out.

"You could always eat her pussy as she's sucking you off while I pump you full." Bryan suggested.

"Fuck, yeah!" Tony said, louder as Bryan tightly pumped him. "Keep going."

"We haven't had a woman together in a while. Don't you want her juices drenching your face right now?" Bryan thrust hard into him.

Tony moaned out, and Bryan knew he was ready for his release. Bryan used both hands to pump Tony's cock as he made long, hard thrusts.

"She could be sucking my cock while you fuck her tight pussy from behind."

That was all it took. Tony's cum shot out as Bryan's own release came. Once the sensitivity was gone, Bryan pulled out and went to the bathroom for a shower. As hot water ran down his back, he heard Tony come in.

"Join me," Bryan called out to him.

Tony stepped in on the opposite end of the large stone shower. As usual, Tony's shower was opposite from his. Bryan liked his water as hot as it would go, where Tony liked his ice cold.

"Alright, let's do it." Tony agreed, as he stepped under the water.

"Do what?" Bryan played dumb.

"Call Gerri. Let's see if she can find us a woman to share." Tony leaned his head back into the shower spray.

"Thought you'd see it my way."

"You paint a good picture." Tony threw cold water at Bryan.

"This will be good for us," Bryan told him. How else would they be complete if they didn't have a woman at their sides? "I'll call Gerri when we get out."

Three

Annette sat at her desk putting in orders for Friday's delivery. She spent most of the day doing inventory for the restaurant she managed. A little bummed, she thought Geri would have called her already. After all, she had Braelynn a date the next day. Maybe she isn't meant to be with a shifter and that's why Gerri hadn't called her. Her cell phone rang, making her jump.

"Hello?" She answered on the second ring.

"Annette? This is Gerri."

"Hi, I was wondering if you forgot about me," Annette admitted.

"I didn't forget," Gerri said. "I needed to make sure I had the right match for you. Sometimes these things take time."

"So, you found a match?" Annette asked.

"Oh, indeed I did. When are you available to meet? Would tonight be too soon?"

"I should be getting off work in about an hour." Annette looked at the clock hanging by the office door. "What time did you have in mind?"

"I'll set you up for reservations at 8:30. How's that sound?"

"Okay, text me the address." Annette didn't want to sound too thrilled.

"Great, the reservation will be under Bryan Steele." Gerri said. "I think you'll enjoy what I've come up with."

By the time she said goodbye, Annette's stomach started fluttering. She was actually going to do this. Her first date with a shifter. She closed her eyes and imagined standing in front of her closet. She wouldn't have much time to get ready, so she needed to have something in mind for when she got home. After mentally picking out two dresses, she focused back on her orders. A few minutes later, her phone chimed with a message. Gerri sent her the address of the restaurant she'd meet Bryan at. Briefly, she wondered what type of shifter he was, then looked up the address on her phone. Skyline, a beautiful skyline restaurant popped up on her screen. *That's definitely not a sports bar.* There won't be any hot wings or darts tonight. She'd have to rethink her attire.

She wasn't able to leave work for nearly two hours. She rushed to her apartment, thankful she only lived fifteen minutes from the restaurant she managed. There was no time to go by a salon so she'd have to make do herself. Once she was in the elevator, she looked at the time on her cell phone. It was almost seven, that didn't give her much time. Why did she agree to do this tonight? She should have put it off until Friday, but then she'd have to cancel because she'd have to be at the restaurant for deliveries. *Suck it up, buttercup.* The moment the elevator doors slid open, she rushed down the hall to her apartment.

For the Love of Fire and Ice

Once in her apartment, she closed the door behind her and twisted the deadbolt. It would be nice if Braelynn was back from her honeymoon to help her pick a dress. She walked into her room, stripping as she went. Originally, she picked out a red dress and a blue dress to try on. Now that she knew her date would be at Skyline, she needed to upgrade her choice. Opening her closest door, she glanced at her wardrobe. She pulled out her deep purple gown. It was formal yet simple. She laid her dress out on the bed and went to shower and shave.

Getting out of the shower, she wrapped a towel around her body and one around her hair. Thankfully her hair wasn't super long, so it wouldn't take long to dry. She went to her dresser to find the sexiest pair of thongs she owned and a matching strapless bra. With her hair still wrapped, she put on her undergarments and went back into the bathroom to blow dry her hair. Once she pulled her hair up, she curled the tips and checked the time. She'd be cutting it close on time, that's for sure. She quickly applied her makeup, and doused her hair with hairspray.

Closing the bathroom door, she looked long and hard in the full-length mirror. It's been a long time since she's been on a real date. Most the time, it was sports bars and night clubs. This would be a good change. If only she had another opinion on her appearance. She wanted to look perfect. Pulling her laptop from her work bag, she opened it up to video chat with Jules. Normally she would just call Braelynn over but she wouldn't be back for a week.

"Come on, Jules. Pick up," Annette spoke while waiting on Jules to accept the chat. Finally, Jules' face popped up on the screen.

"Hi, Annette." Jules waved into the screen.

"I need your opinion." Annette set her laptop down on the bed and took a few steps back. "How do I look?"

"Holy toledo, you look gorgeous," Jules claimed.

"Are you sure? How about my hair?" Annette asked, putting a curl back in its place. The camera on Jules' end began to shake as another figure popped into view.

"Holy moly, Annette! You look stunning," Jules' husband commented.

"Thanks, John." She appreciated a man's input.

"See? I told you," Jules said. "Where are you going?"

"On a real date. No sports bar tonight." Annette laughed. "I'm meeting him at Skyline."

"You look fabulous. Your date is a lucky man," Jules said. "Now get off your computer and go have some fun."

"Thanks, I'll talk to you tomorrow." Annette closed her computer.

She took one final look in the mirror. Nodding her self-approval, she reached into the closet for her black heels. She'd need to hurry if she wanted to make it to the restaurant by 8:30. Switching a few things from her purse to the clutch, she grabbed her keys and left her apartment.

Twenty minutes later, the valet took her car when she arrived at the tall building of the restaurant. She'd never been here before, but Jules and her husband came every couple of months. It's hard to believe Gerri was able to make reservations for tonight at last minute. Jules always had to schedule weeks in advance.

She took the elevator to the top floor. Her reflection in the mirrored doors gave her a chance to put a wayward curl back in place. The soft chime of the elevator sounded just before the doors slid open to a grand foyer leading into the restaurant. Annette ran her hands down her dress, ensuring no wrinkles were seen as she walked up to the hostess podium.

"Welcome to Skyline. Do you have a reservation?" The hostess asked, picking up her pen.

"The reservation is under Bryan Steele," she told the hostess.

"Follow me." She smiled and started walking deeper into the restaurant.

Annette looked around as she followed the hostess. She didn't think Skyline would be this packed on a Tuesday night. A few tables were marked reserved and all the other tables were occupied. As the hostess lead her through, Annette looked for a table with only one gentleman seated but she didn't see any. Most had couples or a group of couples. One table near the rear of the restaurant had two men sitting together. If nothing else, she'll have a good view of those two studs. As the hostess walked closer to the table with the two men, Annette's heart skipped a beat.

"Here you are." The hostess turned and walked away, leaving Annette a little confused. She looked around for a reserved table but there wasn't one marked on this side of the restaurant.

"Annette?" One of the men asked as they both stood and faced her. "I'm Bryan Steele."

"I'm Annette," she said. "But of course you already know that. It's nice to meet you."

"Hello Annette. I'm Tony Glacier." The other man shook her hand and pulled out a seat for her.

Annette was a little taken back. She knew she was going to meet Bryan, but Gerri didn't say someone else would be here, too. Is Tony here for a bail out? Deciding to ride it out, she took the offered seat.

"You look confused," Tony stated.

"I... well, I am honestly. Gerri didn't mention there would be two of you." She might as well put it out there now.

"We're kind of a packaged deal." Bryan chuckled.

"You get one, you get the other too," Tony commented.

Be careful what you wish for. That's what Gerri had told her. She wasn't really expecting two men at once though. What is she going to do with two? A smile broke as she thought of the possibilities of having two men at the same time. It had always been a fantasy. Now, thanks to that godsend of a matchmaker, her fantasy could become a reality.

"This pleases you." Bryan nodded.

"Who wouldn't be pleased?" Annette blushed. "Look at you two."

"He is rather handsome, isn't he?" Tony

asked, nodding towards Bryan.

"Yes, he is," she replied. Then things began to click into place. "Oh, you two are together?"

"We are." Bryan nodded. "We're a bonded pair looking for our third, our female."

"Interesting," she nodded. The possibilities are endless with these two.

"We just haven't found a woman that hits us both in the right ways." Tony winked at her.

"You think Gerri can find such a person," she smiled at them both.

"I think things can get interesting to say the least." Bryan smiled back.

"How did you find out about Paranormal Dating Agency? I didn't think it was wide known to humans." Tony asked.

"Actually, she hooked up my best friend with a shifter. They got married this past weekend." She told them.

"By chance would that be Ronan and Braelynn?" Bryan asked.

"Yeah, how did you know? I would have remembered if either of you had been there."

She asked a little shocked she'd never heard Braelynn mention them. Bryan and Tony looked at each other and smiled, then turned to her.

"We own Heads N' Tails. Braelynn used to come to the club almost daily before she met Ronan. They still come by together," Tony answered.

"She was always trying to get me to go with her. It's just not my scene," she admitted. Braelynn told her about Heads N' Tails. From the way she understood it, it was like a regular club but those that go there are looking for loving. Annette was happy just going out to the local clubs and dancing the night away without expectations. She dated a few guys that enjoyed the scene but that's all she could stand them for. After that, they'd get sloppy and clingy; driving her nuts until she'd explode and dump them.

"How do you know if you've never went?" Tony asked her.

"I went once looking for Braelynn. I was more focused on finding her than what goes on in the club. Other than making sure I wasn't on the menu." She smiled and took a sip of her wine.

"It all depends on which floor you go to," Bryan said. "Before Braelynn met Ronan she'd only been to one floor. There's something for everyone there. We have a fine restaurant similar to this, where dining can be enjoyed under the stars."

"Now that, I could handle." She smiled. She'd been in the restaurant business for most her adult life. "I'd like to see that part one day."

"Once you see one, you'll get curious and want to see the others," Bryan insisted.

"Yeah, just ask Braelynn." Tony laughed.

"She's mentioned it had other floors, but at that time she didn't know what was on them," she said. "The upper level I went to didn't seem like the one Braelynn described."

"Each floor is different."

"I thought it was a sex club for different shifters," she admitted.

"It's much more than that," Bryan told her. "Each floor is different. Humans needed a place where they could cut loose from the world outside and just be free. You can get as adventurous as you want and no one will judge there. Same goes for the other levels. Each one is set up for different beings. Vampires can get fresh blood from donors, without risking illegal blood draining. Though not every floor is in use yet. We're still renovating many levels."

"So what type of shifters are you two?" Annette asked before thinking about if the question was even appropriate.

"We're both dragons," Tony stated.

"Seriously?" She was surprised. "Like big, fire-breathing badasses?"

"Bryan can breathe fire," Tony said.

"You can't?" She asked.

"I'm an ice dragon. I can't breathe fire, though I can freeze anything quicker than liquid nitrogen," Tony bragged.

"Chilling." Annette laughed.

"You have no idea." Tony winked at her.

"This is fascinating," she admitted, as the waitress brought a bottle of wine to the table.

Conversation never slowed as they enjoyed their meal. Bryan and Tony told her about their multi-level club. Bryan offered to give her a tour of their restaurant and she happily accepted. She couldn't believe her luck. Two men just for her. Two fine ass men at that. They had their lives in order. No time for slacking with these two. They had drive and ambition, something that had been missing from her previous boyfriends. She wanted to know everything about them. She'd definitely would like to see them again. The meal went by in a flash; it wasn't enough time.

"Would you like to go dancing?" Tony asked her.

"I'm always ready to go dancing," she replied, eager to spend more time with them.

The waitress brought the check by the table. Bryan placed cash in the check holder as Tony pulled her chair out for her. It was a gentleman's gesture, and she welcomed it.

"Where would you like to go?" Bryan asked her as they each took an arm and escorted her out of the restaurant.

"I thought you may take me to your club."

"Not until you're ready," Bryan assured her.

"I'm ready now." She told him as they stepped into the elevator. "I've been on one of the upper floors, remember? I can handle it. Besides, if we want to continue seeing each other then I'd like to see what I'm getting myself into."

Bryan and Tony looked at each other then smiled over at her. Her heart melted seeing their smiles. They were complete opposites, yet very much the same. She was going to love finding all the differences.

"Please." She turned to face them and ran her hands up their arms. "It would be fun."

"Oh, there's no doubt about that," Tony teased.

"Alright, but be careful what you wish for," Bryan said, as the door to the elevator slid open.

"The last time that was said to me, I got both of you. I'll take my chances." She laughed. She hooked her arms around theirs as they escorted her out.

Tony rode with her in her car as she followed Bryan to Heads N' Tails. Annette hoped they wouldn't be going to the sex crowded levels. A level with good music and good drinks was all she needed for the moment.

Four

Heads N' Tails was bigger than Annette thought possible. She didn't pay much attention when she came with Ronan. Of course, she was pre-occupied with finding out what happened to Braelynn. She had thought that Heads N' Tails was only a couple of levels of the huge building. Instead, she found out every floor of the building was or will be part of Heads N' Tails. Bryan and Tony had spent the last six years transforming the building into a popular place for all types of shifters and paranormal creatures.

"We'll take you to one of the softer levels." Bryan escorted her into the elevator. They didn't even stop by the front desk as she did with Ronan. Then again, when you're with the owners, you don't have to check in.

"Softer levels? What all types of levels are there?" Annette couldn't help but ask.

"There's pretty much anything you could want. There's a level to relax, and shoot a game of pool. Then there's levels where you could get chained to the wall and sexually tortured," Tony said.

"It's whatever your personal preference is," Bryan chimed in.

"How would you know what level to go to?" She asked.

"There's only two ways you can get to any level. You have to be a member or come with a member. There's a membership form we use to help us program membership cards. Take Braelynn for example. On her form, she was anti-shifter, therefore, her membership card would only let her go to the human level. There are no shifters there other than employees. There's also a strict no shift policy in place on that floor," Bryan explained.

"What about the other floors?"

"The rest of the floors cater to paranormals, mainly to shifters. So, the rules aren't as strict," Bryan said.

"We don't have to go in if you don't want to," Tony told her as the elevator stopped and the doors slid open.

"Oh, I want to." Annette took their arms encouraging them to lead the way.

"If it gets to be too much we can always retreat to the penthouse. We definitely have ways of entertaining you there," Tony teased as they stepped off the elevator.

"Like a wall of sexual torture?" She smiled.

"Not on the first date," Bryan assured her, smiling.

"We'll leave that for date number five." Tony held up his hand with his fingers splayed out.

"Tony, don't scare her," Bryan warned.

"Oh, he's fine. I'm not scared at all," she said, hiding all signs of her nervousness.

Annette had expected a level like the one Braelynn had told her about. Where people were practically naked, dancing on each other.

Instead, everyone seemed to have all their clothes on. The dance floor was packed. Annette couldn't blame them; the music had an excellent beat. Tony led the way to the bar. Without waiting for the bartender, Bryan went behind the bar and began mixing up some cocktails.

"Thought you two weren't working tonight?" The bartender called out. Her long purple curly hair swayed as she walked towards them.

"We're not working," Bryan and Tony said in unison.

"We decided to show Annette a little bit of the club," Tony said.

"Plus, show off our skills," Bryan added while shaking the cocktail shaker. "Annette, meet Hannah, one of our best bartenders. She bounces around to different floors each night."

"Until I get my own floor that is." Hannah came over and shook her hand. "Pleasure to meet you."

"Nice to meet you." Annette looked her over trying to figure out what type of shifter she was.

"Hannah wants a pool bar." Tony handed Bryan three cocktail glasses.

"Think about it." Hannah looked at her. "A huge indoor pool with a bar built in, like an island in the center. Some beach music or sounds of ocean waves. There could be UV lights for basking."

"Sounds like a vacation." Annette laughed.

"Hannah's head is full of vacations." Bryan poured the blue concoction into the glasses. "That's why she insists on taking one every month."

"The ocean calls and I must answer." Hannah tossed her purple curls over her shoulder.

"What type of shifter are you?" Annette couldn't contain herself any longer.

"A beautiful mermaid with a shimmering tail that drives all the sailors wild." Hannah swayed her hips to make her point.

"Awesome." Annette was amazed by the different shifters she'd met since Braelynn started dating Ronan.

"Very awesome," Hannah agreed. "I need the ocean's waters to keep me energized, so I spend a few days a month down at the beach."

"Why not just live at the beach? If you love it so much," Annette asked.

"It would seem like the logical thing to do, wouldn't it? It's too dangerous to live out in the open that close to the beach. Monthly trips are enough for now."

"I believe you need to make a trip to the end of the bar." Tony nodded towards a guy waiting with his arms propped up on the bar.

Annette watched Hannah walk over to the man. She could tell there was a story there. Maybe if she and Hannah became friends, she'd hear more of it. Tonight, all her focus was on her dashing dates. They had been perfect gentlemen so far.

Bryan handed them a glass of his fruity concoction. She took a sip, letting the flavors coat her mouth. Usually, she drank wine or beer with the occasional shot thrown in the mix. With this fruity mix, she barely tasted the liquors she watched him pour.

"Wow, this is smooth," she told Bryan.

"Careful, you may not want to drink it fast," he warned.

"I think I'll limit myself with this." She took another sip. "Damn that's good."

"Shall we grab a spot?" Tony held out his hand to her.

She took his hand and looked up at Bryan.

"I don't have another free hand or I'd hold your hand too." She didn't want Bryan to think she was playing favorites.

"That's even better." Bryan slipped up beside her, putting his arm around her waist. "Problem solved."

"Indeed, it is," she agreed as Tony led them through the club.

Annette looked around as she followed Tony. She knew most, if not all, the people here were shifters though they didn't seem any different than her. Everyone was dancing and having a good time. The way Braelynn had described it, she was expecting to see people getting it on right there on the dance floor.

"Not what you were expecting?" Bryan leaned in to her.

"Not exactly." She laughed. She wasn't sure what she had expected, maybe a big orgy on stage. Her thoughts had her laughing again.

"We said we'd bring you to a softer level," Tony pointed out.

"This is about as soft as it gets, other than the restaurant," Bryan told her.

"Guess I was expecting something along the lines of a strip club." She swayed her hips to the music, causing Bryan to sway with her.

"That's on the 21st floor," Tony said with a smile.

"Seriously? You two have it all, don't you?"

"Almost," they said in unison. Tony squeezed her hand as Bryan tightened his grip around her. "We'll have you soon enough. Time is nothing to us."

She loved their confidence. She tried to hide her blush by taking a long sip of her drink. Tony smirked and raised his eyebrow. They came to an empty couch section. Tony held out his hand letting her sit first.

"I still can't believe you two have a strip club here too." She changed the subject.

"There's female and male dancers. Like we said, we like to cater to all types," Bryan said, sitting down next to her.

"To be honest, it's still one of the softer levels too," Tony admitted.

"No one gets chained to the wall?" She teased.

"Not on that level." Tony laughed. "You're hung up on the wall of pleasure, huh?"

"Tony." Bryan glared a warning.

"What?" Tony looked at Bryan then smiled at her. "I bet she'll love it once she tries it."

Her cheeks reddened as heat pooled inside her. A wall of pleasure with these two men excited her more than she cared to express. What could two men do with her all tied up and exposed? Her thoughts raced and she took another sip of her drink. She swayed to the music as she finished her drink.

"I think it's time you two show me what you can do on the dance floor," she stated setting her empty glass on the table.

"Shall I order you another drink and have it waiting for you?" Bryan asked.

"No, we'll grab one later. Right now, I want to dance." Plus, she wasn't fond of unattended drinks.

"You heard the lady, she wants to dance." Tony stood taking her hand in his. Bryan took her other hand and together they led her to the dance floor.

She didn't know how many songs they danced to. She'd never had this much fun dancing with other men. Tony and Bryan passed her between them. With every spin she was in the others arms. When a slow song came on she thought it may get weird, but it didn't. She had her arms around Bryan swaying with the beat. Tony came up behind her with one arm on her belly, and the other sweeping her hair off her neck. He kissed the skin he just exposed as she laid her head against Bryan's shoulder. Halfway through the song Bryan slowly spun her around to finish the song with Tony. They were perfectly in sync with each other.

"It's rare to find a woman that attracts us both," Tony told her softly.

"Your body calls to us," Bryan whispered in her ear. He pressed his body against hers, claiming her neck with his lips.

"What are you going to do about that?" She could barely make out the words as Tony claimed the other side of her neck.

She leaned her head back on Bryan's shoulder giving them both better access to do as they please. It was a bit overwhelming having two men this close.

"Nothing yet," Bryan spoke. "We won't rush you." They both kissed her cheek.

The song faded away and Annette wished for another slow song to play. She didn't want to move from between them. Unfortunately, her wish didn't come true this time. A fast paced, up-beat song came on dashing her dreams of another round on the floor with them.

"You ready for that drink yet?" Tony asked.

No, she thought but simply nodded. She wanted to be back in their arms again. She held their hands as they walked back to the bar for another round of drinks. Bryan went behind the bar to fix them up another cocktail.

"I think this will be my last one. I still have to drive home," she said.

"We got you covered." Bryan handed her another glass.

"You could just stay with us tonight," Tony offered. "We'd like to show you around the penthouse anyways."

Annette smiled thinking about being in their penthouse with them. It would be a great ending to the night.

"I'd like to see your place," she agreed.

Five

"I had a fun time in your club tonight," she told both of them. "Will you bring me back another time?"

"You can come back anytime you want. We'll have a membership card made for you, it will let you go to different floors," Bryan said.

"I don't want to go to all the floors," she told him with wide eyes.

"Don't worry. we'll set it for certain floors, like the ones we're working."

"That will be best, for now at least." She smiled.

The elevator door slid open. As she stepped off the elevator, she was a little confused. It looked like a hallway to a lavish hotel, rather than the penthouse. Bryan and Tony took her hand and led her down the hall.

"I thought you said you live in the penthouse," she commented.

"We have to take a different elevator. Some don't go all the way up. It keeps things separate," Bryan told her. "It gives us an advantage to come up with different designs for the club levels."

"We need to go to the east side elevator to reach the penthouse," Tony explained.

"What are all these rooms?" She asked.

"Just that... rooms. We offer rooms to those who may need one. There's black out rooms incase vampires need a place to stay when daylight comes. Lovers may want a romantic room for the evening. We cater to them all," Bryan said.

"I'd get lost easily."

"Yeah, it's bigger than we expected, too. It leaves room to grow," Bryan admitted.

"Do you have plans for all the floors?" She asked as they came to the eastside elevator.

"Not all of them. It takes some time to convert a floor from rooms into a club," Bryan said.

"We'll get there. Until then we keep the rooms operational," Tony stated and opened a side panel beside the floor buttons.

Annette watched as Tony slid a key card into the elevator keypad then pressed a series of buttons in the panel. As the doors closed, Bryan took her hand, pulling her closer to him. Tony settled in next to them and held her other hand. She looked at Tony then to Bryan. *How did I get myself into this? This is Braelynn's kind of thing, not mine.* Annette was on the verge of panic. *What the hell am I going to do with two?*

"Relax," Tony told her. "We're not going to lock you in a dungeon and take advantage of you."

"Unless you want us to," Bryan laughed and squeezed her hand.

"I didn't think either of you would," she admitted.

"Honey, you have the look of sheer panic in your eyes," Bryan told her. "We can go back downstairs. We're not asking you to jump into bed with us. Just showing you around, that's all."

"It's not that. I just have never had two at once. I'm scared I won't know what to do with you two." The words came out of her mouth without thinking.

"Well, that's the beauty of us. You don't have to do everything. When that time comes, you don't have to worry about pleasing us both at once. You forgot we're bonded. We'll do you and each other," Bryan said with a smile.

"We can give you pleasure together or to each other. Would you like to watch?" Tony raised his eyebrows in a suggestive way.

"That would be interesting." She'd never seen two men together. The thought had her blushing.

A soft ding sounded as they reached the top floor. The doors slid open and Annette was instantly drawn to the entrance foyer. It had stone walls with soft flickering flames of torches on both sides of a large red door.

"Welcome to our little piece of paradise," Bryan said unlocking the door.

"It's looks like a castle." She told him.

"Everything has been customized. From the high vaulted ceiling to the heated floors." Tony said as Bryan opened the door.

Tapestries with Dragon emblems lined the hallway walls on both sides. Each side was decorated a different color. One was a deep brick red with a gold dragon surrounded by flames, and the other a pale blue with a silver dragon in the center with an ice circle around it. Annette reached out to feel the thick tapestry.

"These are beautiful." Annette could imagine their own dragons depicted on the tapestry.

"A little something from home." Tony looked at the ice dragon tapestry.

"Do you miss it?" She asked.

"Sometimes, but this is our home now." Bryan kissed Tony's shoulder. "Come on, we'll give you the tour."

The penthouse was impressive. Every room was nearly the size of her entire apartment. Though the outside entrance made you feel as though you were walking into a castle, the inside was quite modern with an oversized twist. The kitchen was decked out in marble and stainless-steel appliances. A look that she personally loved. A step-down living room was filled with plush furniture that invited you in for a night on the couch. French doors opened up to a large balcony. Wanting to see how high up they were, she stepped out into the cold night's air. The view was spectacular. The clear night let the stars shine bright. The quarter moon gave off a soft glow. She walked to the rail, and looked down. From there she could make out people at the rooftop restaurant a few stories below.

"I thought the restaurant was on the top floor."

"This building has three rooftops. The restaurant is only on one of them. We have a private entrance to the rooftop above us, and the third isn't in use yet. You can see it from the other side," Tony told her.

As if to check his words, Annette went to the opposite end of the balcony and looked over. The other rooftop was closer to them than the restaurant, but it was bare of all people and furniture. She followed them back inside, ready to get back to the tour.

"This is my room," Tony stated as they came closer to a dark blue door with a silver dragon crest in the center.

"I thought you would share a room, since you're bonded and all."

"We do share a room, but we each have a room that's dedicated to our dragons," Tony explained as he opened the door for her to peer inside. "You probably shouldn't go in either of our dragon rooms."

"Why not?" Annette peered inside and immediately knew why it wasn't a good idea.

"Because they're designed for our elements," Tony said opening the door wide.

A chill ran through her. With the door opened wide cold air rushed out causing her to shiver. Everything in the room was iced over. Not that there was much in the room. Pillows littered the ice-covered floor. Annette bent down placing her hand on the floor inside the door. She felt the slick cold ice, and quickly removed her hand.

"How do you keep it that cold?"

"Think of it like a walk-in freezer. My dragon needs the chill factor. Since I couldn't talk Bryan into moving to Alaska, this was the next best thing. I'll take a nap in here while I'm in dragon form. It keeps my dragon happy. I froze the floor myself." Tony told her.

"You have a room like this too?" She asked Bryan.

"My room is much hotter than this." He shivered.

"Is the floor on fire?" She asked with a laugh.

"Nah, that would be a fire hazard for the whole building. It does have heated floors, and heat rocks the size of a couch. Come, I'll show you." Bryan turned on his heel and went to the large brick red door on the opposite side of the living room.

He opened the door and steam rolled out, reminding her of a sauna. A bead of sweat formed on her forehead and she took a step back from the heat. Bryan opened the door wide for her to see inside. Where Tony had pillows, Bryan has heat rocks to lay on.

"Does your dragon nap in here, too?"

"At least twice a week. The rooms are good for our dragons and helps us re-energize much like Hannah and the ocean," Bryan admitted.

"Wanna see where the magic happens?" Tony asked with a devilish grin.

"Of course, I want to see everything." Everything about them intrigued her.

"Follow us." Tony turned and headed down the hall. Bryan closed the door to his room and followed behind them. "One of the bathrooms is through this door. Nothing spectacular, it's mainly for guests."

"Let me guess, the bedroom is through that door." Annette pointed to the end of the hall.

"Good guess," Bryan said coming up beside her.

"This is where all the fun stuff goes down." Tony smiled as he slowly opened the door.

"Wow!" Annette exclaimed as she took a step inside.

The bedroom was just as big as the living room. A huge custom-built bed was against the opposite wall, nearly taking up a third of the space. She'd never seen a bed this size before. How much rolling around room does a dragon shifter need?

"What size of bed is that? I've never seen one that big."

"It's a custom. It has two Emperor mattresses on it." Tony told her. "Feel free to climb on in, if you want." He waved his hand towards the bed.

Whether it was the alcohol she had or the child in her, she had the urge to jump on in. Kicking off her heels, she ran across the room and jumped. She landed on the bed, not as gracefully as she had planned. The skirt of her dress fell half way up her thighs exposing her freshly shaved legs.

"What are you waiting for?" She asked not bothering to fix her dress. "Join me."

Bryan and Tony looked at each other and smiled then ran and jumped on the bed, landing on each side of her. When they landed, it bounced her up. She laughed as she came back down. Blood rushed to her head from the sudden jolt of the bounce.

"Whoa, that was a rush." She laughed. They laughed together and she laid back in the bed.

"Can we kiss you now?" Tony asked her permission.

She nodded and he leaned in, kissing her softly on the lips. Bryan ran his hand down her exposed leg and kissed her neck. Butterflies flittered in her stomach. Tony ran his hand up her other thigh while he deepened the kiss. Tony's kiss was cool, not at all what she had expected. Part of her wondered if it was because he was an ice dragon. Tony pulled back as Bryan turned her head toward him with a finger on her chin. Bryan kissed her with heated passion. His kiss warmed her to the core. She parted her lips, letting his tongue slide over hers.

They took turns kissing, and exploring her body with their hands. She'd give anything to be naked under them. She reached for the buttons on Tony's shirt, unbuttoning one at a time. She pulled off his shirt and turned her attention to Bryan's shirt. She laid back on the bed and admired their bare chests. They took her admiration to the next level when they kissed each other passionately for her viewing pleasure.

"Damn, that's hot!" She reached up caressing both of their chests as they kissed.

"You haven't seen anything yet." Bryan smiled and they turned their attention back on her.

"I think I have too much clothing on," she commented.

"We're just having some fun. Tonight is about getting to know each other. If your clothes come off, then we may not be able to hold back from the things we want to do to you."

"I don't mind." She smiled.

"But we do. You've been drinking and whether you believe it or not, you may be impaired. The first time with us, we want to make sure your conscious is clear. With no regrets," Tony stated.

"My conscious is clear." She pulled her dress up her thigh a little more as if to tempt them into giving in. "No impairment here, just me."

"Another night, we promise." Bryan kissed her shoulder. "Tonight, just let us enjoy you."

"I'm trying to get you to enjoy me." She laughed, trying to hide her disappointment.

"How about a massage instead?" Tony offered.

"I am a sucker for a massage, but how will that work if I'm fully dressed?" She grinned.

"We'll make it work," Bryan assured her.

"Flip over," Tony instructed.

She did as she was told and flipped over onto her belly. She was caught off guard when Bryan hitched her dress up over her ass, leaving her thong clad ass exposed to them. For a moment she was self-conscious. Bryan disappeared from sight but came back quickly with a bottle of massage oil. They positioned themselves on each side of her. All her insecurities left when they put their hands on her. It felt amazing to have their hands massaging her legs.

"You have the prefect body," Bryan said as he caressed his hand at the crease of her ass. His fingers dipped between her legs at the same time Tony's did. She prayed they'd touch her in her special spot. They just barely touched the fabric of her thong then pulled away, leaving her wanting more.

"You're both teases." She grinned.

"No, we're attentive," Tony countered.

"But still a tease," she said.

They laughed and massaged her ass with extra pressure that drove her crazy. She loved the double attention. Her past boyfriends only cared about what she could do for them. It was nice to finally get full attention. The bonus was getting four hands to herself rather than two. Visions of getting Bryan and Tony naked had her body pulsing. Tony's hand slipped under her dress, caressing her hip and dipping a finger in at the crease.

"See? Tease." She laughed.

"Well, I mean if we're going to get accused, we might as well do something." Tony grinned, dipping his finger down once more.

"Keep it up, and you'll be more attentive than you have planned," she grinned.

"Just relax," Bryan told her.

Trying to ignore the fact that she had two sexy men caressing their way up her body. She closed her eyes and relaxed into their touch, trying not to imagine them running their tongues along her skin. She arched her back into their touch.

"You're not relaxing," Bryan warned.

"It's hard to when all I can think about is stripping us down." She smiled into the pillow.

"I think she needs some cooling off." Bryan looked at Tony.

"What does that mean?" She turned toward Bryan.

Tony smiled with a nod. Before she could turn over, Tony blew on her back. The air that past from his lips was as crisp as a winter snowy morning. Her body shivered as the air ran over her body.

"I hope you plan on warming me back up," Annette said to Tony.

"I got that part covered." Bryan smiled and lightly brew warm air down her body. "Now relax."

She turned back over and closed her eyes. Bryan continued to massage her back while Tony's fingers gently slid down her legs. She relaxed on the mattress. Within a few minutes she nodded off to sleep.

Six

Annette woke the next morning, alone, in the gigantic bed. The smell of coffee and bacon were strong enough to come in through the cracks of the closed door. She sat up, letting the sheet fall from around her. Air hit her exposed skin. She looked down wondering when she took her dress off. A red robe sat at the foot of the bed. They must have taken her dress off after she had fallen asleep.

Well, if they've already seen it, why cover up now? She got off the bed, leaving the robe in its place. She walked out the room to look for Bryan and Tony. They were in the kitchen cooking breakfast. Both wearing lounge pants hung low on their hips. She bit her lip as she stepped closer, admiring their bare backs.

"I do love the sight of men cooking," she said, coming into the kitchen.

"Good morning." Bryan turned. His eyes widened as he took in her nakedness. "Wow."

"We made breakfast." Tony turned, dropping a pancake on a plate.

"I appreciate breakfast, but where's my dress?" She asked them, crossing her arms.

"We sent it down to dry cleaning. It wrinkled terribly last night. I put a robe out for you until your dress is ready," Bryan told her.

"You've seen it already. Besides you two are shirtless, I might as well be too." She straightened her shoulders. "Though, I could've sent my dress to the dry cleaners once I got home."

"If you had your dress you would've rushed out this morning. This way you have a reason to stay and spend some more time with us." Tony winked.

"You could've just asked." She laughed.

She took a seat on the bar stool across from their cooking station and watched them prepare the meal. As Bryan fixed their plates, Tony poured orange juice in glasses for them. Bryan balanced the plates on his arms and led the way to the dining table. It wasn't as big as she had imagined, to go with the rest of the penthouse. Instead of a grand table, there was a round hand carved wooden table with four chairs tucked around it. Bryan set the plates down without so much as a wobble.

"You know, if you didn't already own your own restaurant, I'd ask you to come work for me." She took a seat in the chair Tony pulled out for her.

"What if everything goes well, you come work for us?" Bryan countered.

Annette contemplated his offer with a nod. Who knows how far this would go? One thing's for sure, she wasn't about to quit her job without knowing it was for real. Knowing her luck, everything would go great for a bit then they'd aggravate her to the point that she would give up.

She prayed that wouldn't happen. So far, these guys have everything going for them. What could go wrong?

"Breakfast was delicious. The bacon was perfectly cooked," she complimented.

"Thank you," they said in unison.

"When can we see you again?" Bryan asked and Tony kicked him from under the table.

"I'm not even gone yet," she laughed. She'd love to see them both again.

"I know," Bryan started, "I figured we'd have another date and show you our restaurant."

"I'd like that. I won't get off work until late tonight, though."

"Time doesn't matter," Bryan insisted. "Even the restaurant is open every day, day and night."

"Okay, it's a date." She smiled. Even practically nude, she was comfortable with them.

"Great, it's settled. Tonight, we dine," Bryan declared.

"First, I shower," Tony stated, gathering up the plates. "Care to join? It's big enough for you to have your own water spray."

"Since It's big enough." She really just wanted to see them naked.

*****

The bathroom was nearly the size of the bedroom. The shower had more than enough room to fit six people inside. Six main shower heads sprayed hot water down on them. Tony had to show off the other features of the shower by turning a dial on the shower wall. Massaging jets of water hit her from the sides. Annette turned her back to the jets, letting the water massage her back.

"I wish my apartment had water pressure like this." She leaned back into the water, letting it pour down her body. When she opened her eyes, Bryan and Tony were staring at her. With their smoldering looks, she knew they liked what they saw.

"You have the body of a Goddess," Tony remarked.

"I wouldn't go that far," she replied. Never had she been compared to a goddess.

"I would," Bryan commented. "You're fucking perfect."

Annette ran her hands down her body. She'd never been ashamed of her body, even if she did have some extra weight in some spots. She was proud of every inch. She watched as they turned to wash up. Soap suds ran down Bryan's ass cheek, and Annette bit her lip. She'd love to get her hands on his ass. Water ran down Tony's back, and she couldn't stand it any longer. She had to get her hands on them. How could they resist her with no clothes on? She hoped they couldn't as she left her shower head and walked up behind Tony.

"You missed a spot," she told him, taking the soap from his hand.

"Did I?"

She could see his grin as he looked over to Bryan. She lathered the soap in her hands then handed it back to him. With her fingers splayed out, she ran her soapy hands down his back. He wasn't in bodybuilder shape, but his muscles were well toned. She ran her hands along his back, taking in the feel of his body. She tilted her head and watched the bubbles slid down his ass cheeks. *Damn, that's sexy.* How could she find two more perfect men?

"I missed a spot you can get." Bryan turned his back to her.

Tony handed her the soap, and smiled. They weren't in competition with each other. She could tell they both enjoyed it. She lathered up her hands and handed the soap back. She washed Bryan's back with the same dedication as she did Tony's. Bryan stood a few inches shorter than Tony but was still a few inches taller than her. She ran her hands along his back, watching the trail of bubbles run down his body. Tony stepped up behind her. His soapy hands caressed her shoulders. Soap suds streamed down her breast.

"That's sexy," she thought she heard Tony whisper in her ear.

She turned her head, but he was standing straight. He grinned and slid his hands slowly down her back. He didn't stop at her waist. His hands caressed her ass, sending her body into delight. Tony stepped back, and water rinsed her back.

Bryan adjusted the shower head, letting the water rinse the soap away. He turned toward her, looking at her from head to toe. Water drops littered his shoulder as he took steps closer to her.

"Such beauty," Bryan said as he leaned in pressing his lips against hers.

She waited until he deepened the kiss to wrap her arms around him. Her breast pressed against his wet skin. Tony kissed her shoulder. She reached behind Tony, grabbing his ass. She pulled him in closer to her, sandwiching herself between them. They're bodies reacted to hers. Tony's hard cock rested between her ass cheeks. Her muscles clenched at the thought of him being inside her.

She broke away from her kiss with Bryan. Tony kissed her neck, and she turned her head towards him. Her lips met his. He brought his hand to her cheek to deepen the kiss. Bryan kissed a trail down her neck to her breasts. He gently teased her hard nipples as he took her breasts into his hands. Before she could get a kink in her neck, she broke off the kiss. Facing Bryan, she ran her hands along his chest. His nipple ring was calling to be toyed with. She leaned forward and kissed his neck and worked her way down to his nipple. She flicked his nipple ring with her tongue. Her hands moved down his abs, feeling each ridge of muscle.

Tony's arm wrapped around her, slipping his hand between her legs. Her body shook as he explored her most sensitive area. Bending over she ran her tongue down Bryan's abs. She wrapped her hand around his erection. Continuing the trail south, she took him into her mouth. Tony got down on his knees behind her. She spread her legs apart and arched her back, giving Tony an open view. He spread her folds and explored her with his tongue.

"Fuck, that's hot," Bryan said, looking down at them.

'Bite down baby,' it sounded as if he was

right by her ear, but it was muffled. She smiled and bit down. She lightly scraped her teeth along his shaft. Bryan moaned out in pleasure.

"Tony, show her the pleasures in having us both." Bryan said, leaning back against the shower wall. As Tony stood, she looked back to see what he was doing.

"You keep going, baby." Tony stroked her back with his hand as he positioned himself behind her. "We want to fill you from both ends."

She took Bryan's hard cock back into her mouth, swirling her tongue around the head. Tony teased her with his cock, brushing it against her but not going in. When he was centered over her core she pushed back onto him, taking him in inch by inch.

"Oh hell," Tony moaned.

Bryan's cock swelled with excitement. She pumped his cock to match her rhythm with Tony. Her lips would meet her hand with each thrust. Their moans gave her great pleasure to know that she could please two at once. As Tony filled her from behind, her walls stretched to accommodate his size.

'*Harder,*' she thought, wanting to be forced on Bryan.

Tony's hand gripped her hips. He thrusted into her with enough force she was deep throating Bryan's cock. As if he had read her mind, his thrust reached the depths of her. Each thrust was slow but powerful. Bryan's cock went to her throat, slowly she was pushed further then brought back off in time with Tony. Her clit throbbed with her building release. Tony reached around her, circling her clit with his fingers. Her body quaked with her release as Tony pushed deep inside. Bryan's cum shot down her throat, and she swallowed on reflex. Tony pounded into her once more as he came inside her. He held her to him as she pulled Bryan's cock from her mouth. When she stood up, Tony slowly pulled out of her and kissed her shoulder.

"That was new," she commented.

"You've never swallowed?" Bryan asked.

"No." She laughed. "I've never had two men

at once."

"I'm positive it won't be the last." Tony smiled as he stepped back under the shower head.

"It's definitely something I'd love to do again." Bryan brushed his lips against her with a soft kiss. "Next time, I get that tight pussy." He reached around and squeezed her ass.

"You can have whatever you want," she told him. She realized then she meant it. She'd let these two do whatever they wanted to her body. She knew it would be nothing but pleasure.

"Good, then we'll continue this tonight," Bryan said.

They quickly washed again then stepped out of the shower. Just as she wrapped a towel around her body, a bell rung out in the hallway.

"Your dress is back." Tony slipped on his robe and left the bathroom.

Twenty minutes later she was heading back to her apartment to get ready for work. She couldn't stop smiling. *Today will be a good day,* she thought. With a start like that, nothing could bring her down.

Seven

"See, I told you calling Gerri was a great idea," Tony said as the elevator door closed.

"Annette is perfect," Bryan admitted. "She's the one. She heard my thoughts of what I wanted. She can read us."

"I can definitely read her." Tony smiled.

"She didn't say anything about it. Do you think she knows?" Bryan asked.

"She probably didn't even realize it happened," Tony stated. "She may have thought you were talking. It's not like she was looking at your face."

"I was looking at hers. Did you see her cheeks hollow when she sucked my cock? Damn, that was amazing."

"More amazing than my blowjobs?" Tony teased.

"I say she'll give you a run for your money, but no one could replace your lips." He leaned over and kissed Tony, as to bring the fact home.

"I never thought she could replace me. As long as she makes you happy, I'm happy."

"You know she makes you happy, too. When was the last time a female made your eyes roll back when you came?" Bryan crossed his arms. "Don't worry, I'll wait."

"Well, it's not about me. It's about us," Tony said. "Every part of me wanted to claim her as ours. She won't get jealous of us, either. She'll embrace it."

"I hope you're right." The elevator stopped on the twelfth floor. "I'll see you tonight." Bryan gave Tony a kiss before stepping off the elevator.

*****

Days flew by. They spent each night with Annette. Once they took her to their restaurant it had become her favorite place to dine. Besides the restaurant, they had taken her to three different levels of the club. She drew the line at the naughtier levels. At the end of the night, she'd come back to their penthouse, claiming her apartment complex was lonely with Braelynn on her honeymoon.

"It's Saturday night. Where should we take her?" Tony asked grabbing a bottle of water from the refrigerator.

"I was going to try and talk her into going to level 15," Bryan said.

"You think she's ready. She already drew the line at naked bodies all over the place."

"Maybe she'll feel differently about this one. The only ones naked are the performers. I think she'll enjoy it once she gets in there and gets a drink in her hands."

"You better make it a strong one." Tony laughed. "Oh, and since this was your idea, you can ask her."

"She'll be fine. She has more kink in her than she's letting on."

"That's for damn sure," Tony agreed.

Bryan's cell phone rang, breaking into their conversation. He held a finger up, letting Tony know they'll continue in a minute.

"Hello?" He answered.

"Dar-ling, has my smoldering rock cooled his heels?"

"Mara?" Bryan couldn't believe she was calling him after all these years.

"Yes, darling. It's me."

"What do you want Mara?" He asked already irritated by the sound of her voice.

"I want you to come back to Nova Aurora. It's time to put this nonsense behind you and come home where you belong."

"This is my home. I'm not going back." He looked to see where Tony was. As Tony took a few steps closer, Bryan held up his hand. *It's okay,* he told Tony.

"I gave you time to play out your little fantasy trip." Her voice gritted on his nerves.

"It's not a fantasy trip for me, but you need a reality trip," he told her.

"The reality is, you need to get your butt back to Nova Aurora. You'll forget all about Tony once you're back home."

"The reality is I chose Tony."

"Tony can't bare your children. We both know that's what you want in the end anyway. A bunch of children carrying your fire blood. I can give you that. Our children will be strong."

"Don't you worry about my future children. Tony and I have decided together, and believe me when I tell you it's not you."

"Bryan Steele, you get your ass," Mara began to rant again. Not feeling up to hearing her anymore, Bryan hung up before she could even finish her sentence.

"Damn, that woman is aggravating." Bryan put the phone down on the kitchen counter.

"Why would she call now? It's been over six years. How'd she get your number?" Tony asked.

"It's only been months for her on Nova Aurora. I don't know how she got my number. It doesn't matter though. I choose you today, the same as I did back then. Mara would never accept us, so I can't accept her. Besides, we have someone who is perfect for us both. Annette is the one we want and need. Not a crazy bitch that can't stand the sight of us being in the same room together."

"Good, because I don't think my dick would even get hard for that evil bitch," Tony admitted with a laugh.

"Let's not mention this to Annette," Bryan suggested.

"I think she already knows," Tony said. "I've had that tingling connection feeling since you were on the phone. If the connection was through me then she doesn't know what Mara was saying, just you."

"And now?" Bryan asked.

"No, it stopped. I wouldn't be surprised if she heard everything."

"Well, I'm not mentioning it unless she brings it up."

"That's fine by me." Tony shrugged. "I don't think she would care though."

"Maybe not. She'll be coming up here around ten o'clock. What floor you working?" Bryan asked.

"I'll be down with the humans until Kalene comes in at eight."

"So, you won't be getting off until nine." Bryan snorted.

"No, she knows not to be late. One more strike and she's out," Tony said.

"That's the problem with human bartenders. They drink on the job and they're too hungover to make it in on time the next day."

"We need a full-time shifter down there," Tony suggested.

"Kade has a couple guys that might be right for the job. I'll check with him next week." Bryan grabbed a water from the refrigerator. "I'll be down in construction until seven."

"I'll see you at home then." Tony kissed his cheek and left for the elevator.

After Tony left, Bryan looked at his phone. Where did Mara call from? The number on the screen was blocked, so he had no way of knowing where the hell Mara was. He just hoped it was far away from them. He left her years ago because she hated the fact that he loved Tony. She made it clear she wouldn't tolerate him being with another, especially a man. The decision to leave came easy, Tony tipped the love scale a lot more than Mara. She had to go. Bryan thought by coming to Earth, he would be free from Mara's evil schemes. Though if she called his cell phone then she had to be around somewhere.

Eight

"I'm not going crazy, Braelynn," Annette said into the phone. "I swear I heard them talking and they weren't in the room. Hell, they aren't even in the building."

"It's not crazy. I hear Ronan all the time," Braelynn said.

"You're married though. You're supposed to have that bond." She stabbed her fork into the lettuce on her plate.

"How long has it been going on?" Braelynn asked.

"I don't know. I think from the start. It's not always clear," she told her. "I accidently eavesdropped on their conversation today."

"Annette, that's an invasion of privacy," Braelynn warned.

"It's not like I could help it. I don't know how to make it stop," she admitted with frustration.

"You can't stop it. Hold on a minute." Annette heard muffled voices, like Braelynn covered the phone. "Ronan says with a lot of practice you can block it or make it stronger."

"Okay, and just how do I do that?" She checked the time on her phone and took a bite of her salad.

"Hell, I don't know. You'll have to ask your boyfriends."

"That sounds strange," she admitted.

"I can't believe I leave you alone and within a week you have two men pining for you."

"Right? Crazy huh?" She could still hardly believe it herself.

"What's crazy is you being cool with the fact that I've been with Tony."

"No offense honey, but I think you've slept with most of the men around here at one point or another." She laughed.

"Yes, well now we won't have to worry about that. Ronan is plenty enough for me." Braelynn giggled, no doubt Ronan was messing with her.

"I'm glad Gerri found him for you," Annette admitted. She was truly happy for her Braelynn.

"Me too."

"So, when are you coming back?" She asked, picking a cucumber out of her salad and taking a bite.

"We'll be back tomorrow. Hey, you want to come over for a packing party?" Braelynn asked.

"Oh, you mean, will I come over and help you pack your shit while we get shitfaced on wine?"

"Well… yeah." Braelynn laughed.

"Yeah, I'm off tomorrow. Just give me a call when you get back in town." Annette agreed.

"You going on another date tonight?"

"Yeah, I'll swing by their place when I get off work." She looked at the time again. "Speaking of work, my lunch break is just about over. Call me tomorrow."

"Alright, talk to you tomorrow."

"Have a safe trip." Annette hung up with Braelynn and shoved the last of her salad in her mouth.

Just a few more hours and she'd get to see her men. Every time she thought of them she got flutters in her stomach. How did she get lucky enough for two? They've shown her incredible pleasure. Everything they've done has been with thoughts of her first. Neither has argued over who gets her time. Last night, Tony ended up working a couple of extra hours. She spent that time with Bryan and Tony joined them when he got off. With three in the relationship, it didn't feel awkward like she thought it would. They were in perfect harmony together.

It was just after ten o'clock when she made it to Heads N' Tails. Bryan gave her an access keycard so they wouldn't have to escort her up every time she came over.

"Hi Annette," Tyra greeted her. "Did you get in touch with Bryan?"

"Why? Is something wrong?"

"No, remember you called to get his number because you lost your phone?" Tyra looked confused, which mirrored the expression on her own face.

"Tyra, I didn't call you today," she told her. Annette reached in her pocket for her phone. "My phone is right here. It's been with me all day."

"You didn't?" Tyra asked.

"Nope, whoever it was, wasn't me," she replied.

"Oh shit," her eyes widened. "I'll probably get chewed out for it then."

"It's no big deal. Just tell him it was a mistake."

"Easy for you to say. You're not the one who made the mistake." Tyra sighed.

"Don't worry, I'll leave him in a happy mood." She smiled and headed to the elevator.

"You do that," Tyra called out as the elevator door closed.

She remembered the guys wondering how a woman named Mara got Bryan's phone number. *Guess that mystery is solved.* From the conversation she overheard earlier, neither Tony nor Bryan liked the woman very much. For a moment, she considered asking them about her, but the moment passed as quickly as it came. They'll tell her when they're ready. With the animosity they seem to have for the woman, Annette knew she had nothing to worry about. Besides they already claimed that they wanted her and not that Mara chick. That was good enough for her.

Once she got off the main elevator, she needed to follow the hall around to the east elevator. When she turned the corner, a tall redhead stepped off the elevator. The woman had on a tight black leather dress. The woman looked amazing except for her nose being stuck up in the air. She eyed Annette as she passed. Something seemed strange about the woman. *Maybe she has something against humans.* Annette had to remind herself that she was in shifter land up here. She hadn't had a bad feeling about being on the shifter floors. Being with Tony and Bryan made her feel safe. She was getting to know a few of their employees, and she always took the same route to the penthouse. She wouldn't venture off the beaten path unless with her shifters.

Before getting into the elevator, Annette looked back down the hall. The hall was clear when she stepped into the elevator. She copied everything she had seen Tony do with the side panel. She felt at ease the moment the elevator started moving.

The soft ding alerted her that she arrived on the penthouse floor. As the door slid open, movement caught her eye causing her to jump and throw her hand up.

"Sorry love." Bryan reached for her. "I was coming down to see if you had gotten lost."

"I ran a little late at work," she said, stepping off the elevator and straight into Bryan's embrace. "Where's Tony?"

"He'll be up in a few. He's in the process of firing one of our employees." Bryan took her hand and escorted her into the penthouse.

"That's terrible," she said. "Do you have coverage for the position?"

"Yeah, Hannah came in to cover for tonight." Bryan looked over at her and smiled. "Why? Would you like the job?"

"Ha," she sat down on the couch. "I can cover while a bartender is on break, but for a whole night? Not a chance."

"Well, it was worth a try." He laughed as he sat beside her.

"He couldn't talk you into it, could he?" Tony came in through the door.

"A bartender, I am not." She smiled up at Tony.

"Huh?" Tony's eyebrow arched in a quizzical look.

"I offered her Kalene's job. I was only joking though," Bryan chimed in.

"What else was he going to talk me into?" She asked Tony but raised her brow at Bryan.

"I wanted to ask you over a nice glass of wine," Bryan started.

"Hold on," Tony went to the kitchen. He was

only gone for a minute before returning with three wine glasses filled with red wine. "Now, you can continue."

"Why do I have a feeling this is a loaded question?" She smiled and took a sip of wine.

"You see, I was thinking you may like to see a different level of the club tonight." Bryan paused.

"I'm listening," she urged him to continue.

"I want to take you to level 15."

"What's on 15?" She asked.

"You'd have to see it to appreciate it," Tony said taking a seat beside her.

"I guess the best way to explain it to you is, theatre meets strip club."

"As long as you promise no one will be grinding on me."

"The only one to grind on you is us," Tony stated.

"Woah, is that a hint of jealousy?" She teased Tony.

"We may share you, but it doesn't go outside our circle," Tony said. "They can look all they want. We're the only ones allowed to touch."

"I'm totally okay with that." She smiled. Two is all she could handle.

"So, you'll go?" Bryan asked.

She thought about it for a moment. They wouldn't let anything happen to her. She put her trust in them before when it came to the different levels of their club. They knew her limits and she doubted they would take her anywhere she'd be uncomfortable.

"I'll go anywhere with you two," she admitted.

"Great!" Bryan leaned over and kissed her cheek.

"Have you eaten yet? We can swing by the restaurant on our way down," Tony asked. "They also serve food on the theatre level, mainly appetizers."

"I had a large salad at work, so I should be good," she answered.

"We'll fix a midnight snack when we get back," Tony suggested.

"Sounds good."

They sat around on the couch, talking about

their day, and finishing their wine. Neither Bryan nor Tony mentioned the call from Mara.

"Is there a time we need to be downstairs?"

"No, the performances continue through the night. I figured we'd mosey on down when you finish your wine," Bryan told her.

"In that case." She finished the last sip of her wine.

Bryan collected their empty glasses and took them to the kitchen. Before leaving she needed to make a quick stop to the bathroom. She looked into the mirror and checked her makeup. Her hair was still pinned up in a twist. She pulled the pins out, letting her hair fall just passed her shoulders. After finger brushing her hair, she left the bathroom.

"Ready?" Tony asked, offering her an arm. She grabbed her purse from the kitchen counter.

"Ready as I'll ever be." She hooked her arms around theirs as they left the penthouse.

Nine

The theatre level was larger than she thought possible for being on the 15th floor. Bryan explained to her how they combined the 15th and 16th floors to give it the high ceilings and raised seating. The stage could easily hold a large orchestra. Though it wasn't the size of the stage that drew her attention, it was the beautiful woman dancing on stage. Her body resembled that of a human, but her coloring was different. There was a green tint to her skin. Green scale like spots lined her face and neck. Her lean body was barely covered by a sheer white dress. Her seductive dance was captivating. She radiated beauty as she gracefully moved across the stage. Annette couldn't take her eyes off the dancer. She danced around the stage, looking around at the audience. Her eyes shone bright yellow when she looked Annette's way.

"Don't stare into her eyes," Tony whispered in her ear. When she didn't look away, he stepped in front of her and planted his lips on hers. Instantly, she was drawn into his kiss and closed her eyes.

"What was that?" Her voice was barely above a whisper.

"That was Giana," Tony replied.

"I forgot she was up tonight." Bryan led them to a table near the center of the room.

"Giana is a bit mysterious," Tony said, pulling a seat out for her. "We know she's a serpent, just not sure exactly what. Lock gazes with her and you'll be drawn to her. A crush as you would say."

"The allure is more appealing to humans." Bryan took a seat next to her.

"Got it, don't look into her eyes." Annette figured that would be easy. She has better eyes to look at. "Thank you for saving me from a girl crush," she told Tony.

"Not a problem. There's only room for one woman in this relationship." Tony smiled.

"Don't worry. I don't want to see you two with another woman. You two are mine," she declared.

Bryan smiled over at Tony. "Told you, she's the one." She heard Bryan speak but his mouth wasn't moving. What Braelynn said was true. These were the men for her.

Giana was still performing on stage. Annette watched the performance while avoiding looking at her face. As her dance came to an end, many clapped their hands. A few gentlemen whistled out. A loud roar sounded from the back of the room. Annette jumped and quickly looked around for the source of the roar. A man with sandy blonde hair sat on the far side of the room. He's face was elongated to that of a lion. She watched as it slowly turned back into a man's face.

"He's not going to turn into a lion right here in the room, is he?" She asked them.

"It's not likely," Bryan said. "Yet, we don't

have to hide who we are here."

"We created this place specifically for shifters," Tony added.

"Then why have a human level at all?"

"Who are we to discriminate? Humans need love, too." Tony winked.

"Beings of all kinds need a place where they can be themselves. A place to unwind from the outside world," Bryan said.

Bryan's body stiffened. He stared off behind her with narrowed eyes. Annette turned in her seat to see what or who he was focused on. There were too many people for her to tell exactly who he was looking at. No one was looking in their direction. Most were focused on the performers coming out on stage.

"Excuse me, loves." Bryan got up from his seat. "I'll bring back some wine."

Annette watched as Bryan walked toward the bar, but her view was cut off by two couples slowly making their way to their own seats. When Bryan came back into view he was talking to the tall red head, she had seen in the hallway earlier.

"Is that Mara?" Annette asked Tony, turning back to face him.

"So, you did hear us." Tony smiled.

"Only a little," she admitted.

"Yeah, that's Mara," he said, looking just as irritated as she felt with Mara's appearance. "She's from Nova Aurora."

"Then, why is she here?"

"She wants Bryan to go back," he said simply.

"Tough shit," Annette spat out. "That shouldn't be up to her. Clearly, Bryan chose not to be there for whatever reason."

"He left for me," he told her. "Their parents wanted them to marry. A family merger so to speak. They dated for a while. She just couldn't accept that a woman alone couldn't complete him. She wouldn't accept a man in the same bed with them."

"Man, she doesn't know what she's missing." Annette leaned over and kissed him softly.

"You have the softest lips," he spoke as she pulled back.

"I leave for five minutes and you're already stealing all the kisses." Bryan smiled at them.

"There's plenty more where that came from. Come here and I'll show you."

Bryan set the wine glasses down on the table, one in front of each of them. She pulled Bryan close and pressed her lips against his. His tongue ran across her lips. Her lips parted and invited him in. All too soon, he pulled back from the kiss.

"There's more for later, too." She winked.

"Good to know." Bryan kissed her cheek.

"Why is Mara here?" Tony asked. Bryan's eyes widened, and he looked over to Annette.

"I already know about her," she admitted. Bryan sighed and closed his eyes for a moment before opening them again.

"She said she's here visiting her brothers. They recently moved here, and she's staying with them for a while. We may have to put up with her from time to time."

"I thought you had to have a membership to get in here." Annette commented.

"Members are allowed to bring a guest. I'll have her brothers' membership flagged. We'll know when they bring a guest next time," Bryan explained.

"I was always under the impression her brothers didn't like her much," Tony commented.

"Half-brothers," Bryan corrected. "As far as I know, they don't. Things can change, I guess."

Annette picked up her wine glass to take a sip. As she brought the glass to her lips, she felt a jerk and wine spilt down her blouse.

"Shit!" She set the glass back down on the table and looked around to see who tipped her glass. She didn't see anyone walking by or standing near their table.

"What happened?" Tony asked as Bryan handed her a cloth napkin.

"I'm a klutz," she said. "Where's the restroom? I need to get cleaned up."

"It's over there," Bryan pointed to a hall on the left side of the room. "Follow the hall, it's the first door on the right."

"Thanks, I'll be back in a minute." She stood

and grabbed her purse.

"I'll escort you." Tony went to stand, but she placed her hand on his shoulder.

"I got it. I won't be gone long." She grabbed the cloth napkin to take with her.

She went straight to the bathroom, avoiding making eye contact with anyone. The restroom was easy enough to find. She set her purse down on the counter next to the sink and turned on the water. Wetting the corner of the napkin she dabbed at the red wine stain.

"Ugh!" She said in frustration. "This is never going to work."

She dropped the napkin by the sink with a frustrated sigh. Gripping the bottom of her blouse, she pulled it over her head. Suddenly, a clattering echoed through the restroom. She pulled her head out of her blouse and looked around the restroom. No one was there. Her purse and all its contents laid strewn out across the floor.

"Lovely, just fucking lovely." She threw her blouse down by the sink.

She crouched down and picked up her purse. She didn't think she had set it that close to the edge. One by one, she picked up her stuff and shoved it back in her purse. Her wallet made it all the way over to a stall. The restroom door opened and Annette jerked her head around to see the doorway empty. Finally retrieving everything, she stood up placing her purse farther back on the table. She turned the water off, not even in the mood to try and save her blouse. Thankfully, she had on a spaghetti strap tank top underneath. The wine only seeped through a little. It shouldn't be too noticeable under the dim lights of the club. Finally accepting her ruined attire, she shoved her blouse in her purse and left the restroom.

On her way back to the table, she recognized Mara heading in the same direction. Irritation fueled Annette as she picked up her pace to cut Mara off. Why won't she just go away? She stepped in front of Mara a few feet from where Bryan and Tony were enjoying the performance on stage.

"Just where do you think you're going?" Annette put her hand out to stop Mara.

"I'm going to talk to Bryan," Mara stated with her nose turned up.

"I'm sure you already bothered him enough for one night."

"What do you know of it?" Mara snarled.

"I know Bryan made his choice clear, and it's not you."

"What you think it's you?" Mara laughed.

"You damn right it's me." Annette smiled.

"Doubtful," Mara said. "You're just as pathetic as Tony. Why don't you two run along and play? Let Bryan have a real woman."

Annette had had enough from today, and she'd had enough of Mara. Usually she could keep herself in check but the moment Mara insulted Tony, that was it. Annette balled up her fist. Without batting an eye, she punched Mara square on the lip.

"Oh shit!" Tony said as he and Bryan jumped from their seats.

A big burly man wrapped his arms around Mara before she could throw a punch. Bryan grabbed Annette's arms, holding them down by her side.

"You better watch out girlie," Mara spat out, blood dripping from her lip. "You have no clue who you're fucking with."

"I see a desperate bitch, who doesn't know when to let go." Annette pointed to her lip, in the spot that mirrored Mara's busted lip. "I think it's time to let go."

"I'll see you again," Mara grunted out as the burly man pulled her away.

Annette watched as Mara was escorted from the club. Hopefully, she'd leave for good. Though, Annette could bet she'd be seeing Mara again.

"Why did you do that, love?" Bryan asked turning her to face him.

"She had it coming." Annette shrugged. "She shouldn't have insulted Tony."

Tony and Bryan both laughed and engulfed her in a hug.

"Sorry, I started a fight in your club." She winced.

"Are you kidding me?" Tony said, looking at her. "That was fucking sexy."

"Not very smart, but sexy," Bryan agreed.

"Well, I'm not going to let her run off at the mouth. Someone had to shut her ass up."

"You truly are remarkable," Bryan commented, kissing her forehead. "I don't think I have ever seen a human challenge a dragon shifter."

"I wasn't challenging her," she said. "Well, maybe I was. She can't go around messing with my men."

"Oh, I think she got the message." Tony laughed.

"Good, now let's enjoy the show." Annette took her seat back at the table.

For the first time since coming out of the restroom Annette looked to the stage. The performance was an interpretive dance between a woman and two men. She watched with infatuation as the two men fought over the beautiful dancer. The woman's dress was ripped from her body as the men pulled her from each side. Her naked body was on display for everyone to see. Annette couldn't take her eyes away. She'd never thought of herself as a voyeur but she had to admit, the scene before her was turning her on.

"Told you there's a freak in there." Bryan squeezed her thigh and smiled over at Tony.

"No doubt," Tony agreed.

"I am not," she objected.

"Love, there's so much freak in you, it's dying to come out. How else would you have gotten the two of us?" Tony winked.

"Hmm," she thought about it for a second. "You may have a point there."

"How's your hand feeling?" Bryan picked up her hand and examined her knuckles.

"Sore at the moment, but it'll be okay."

Tony grabbed one of the cloth napkins off the table. He blew onto the napkin, holding it inches from his lips. She could hear the crackling as it frosted over. He took her hand in his, covering her knuckles with the cloth. She hissed out the moment the intense cold touched her already swollen knuckles. After a few seconds her hand adjusted to the cold.

"Thank you." She kissed his cheek. "I bet that skill comes in handy."

"We never need ice." He smiled.

"Oh, this is the best part," Bryan commented, drawing their attention to the stage.

"Who will she choose tonight?" Tony asked.

"It's not always the same?" She asked.

"Nope, they always perform together but which man she gets is a surprise for the audience each night."

"Looks like she'll have them both. Smart girl," she watched the sexual dance unfold before her eyes.

The woman jumped into one man's arms, wrapping her legs around him. As she slid down onto his cock, the other man came up behind her. He centered himself on her ass and together both men filled her at once. It was one thing that Annette hadn't done with Tony and

Bryan. She hadn't seen them together either. Which if she was honest, was something she was dying to see.

"Giving you dirty little ideas?" Bryan grinned.

"Actually, I was thinking about a different little three-way," she hinted. "Personally, I think we should go back upstairs. I've had enough fun for one night."

"By all means, let's go. We can't have you getting bored on us." Tony smiled.

"Oh, I didn't say anything about being bored. I just have other things on my mind." She squeezed their thighs then winced as pain shot up her hand.

All three stood in unison. She grabbed her purse and slid it over her shoulder. Bryan and Tony each offered her an arm. She wrapped her arms around theirs as they left the club. She half expected Mara to be out by the elevators, but the hallway was empty.

✶✶✶✶✶

Once they got back to the penthouse, Bryan took her blouse to try and get the stain out while Tony grabbed a bandage wrap for her hand. It warmed her heart to see these two men taking care of her.

"Is your hand feeling any better?" Tony asked as he secured the wrap around her hand. He gave the top of the wrap a light blow. It cooled on her hand.

"It'll get there, thanks."

"It's the least I could do since you were defending my honor."

"She had no right telling Bryan who he should or shouldn't be with. I believe people should be free to do as they wish, with who they wish," she told him. "If Bryan didn't want to be with us then I'm sure he would say it."

"Believe me, that is the furthest thing from his mind." Tony blew a kiss in Bryan's direction.

"Volia," Bryan held her blouse up. She could barely even tell the red wine had been there other than the huge wet spot where he had been cleaning it. "Now we'll just run it through the washer and no one will ever know."

"How did you do that?" Annette asked amazed. "I can't believe it came out without an hour of soaking."

"Easy, just dish detergent and peroxide," Bryan claimed. "I'll throw it in the washer."

"You two surprise me all the time," she admitted to Tony.

"I hope we can continue to surprise you," he said tucking her hair behind her ear.

"Now, that that's done," Bryan came back into the living room. "I think we should get you to the bedroom and strip all your clothes off."

"That does sound like a delightful idea." She giggled and jumped from the couch.

She ran to the bedroom with them hot on her heels. They caught her just as she reached the bed though she knew they could have easily caught her any time they wanted. They all fell down onto the bed laughing. As she was about to sit up, Bryan grabbed the bottom of her tank top and yanked it over her head. He eased her arm out, so it wouldn't hurt her hand. Tony unbuttoned her pants and with each one grabbing a pants leg, they slid them off. All she was left in was her black lace bra and matching thongs.

"Damn, look at that body," Bryan said. "Looks good enough to eat."

"Then why don't you?" Annette grinned. She loved they way their tongues felt against her body.

Each took a side of her, sitting down beside her. Their hands ran along her body, massaging her as they did the first night. She unbuttoned their shirts one at a time as they explored her body with their hands. They stood and stripped down. As she reached back to unclasp her bra, Tony shook his head.

"That's my job," he kicked off his pants and got back on the bed.

Annette stayed on her elbows so she could watch as they had their way with her. Tony kissed along her belly, moving his way to her breast. Bryan kissed his way up her thighs. He blew warm air on her body as he moved to the fabric of her thongs. His hands moved to the waist line of her thongs and pulled them down her legs. Tony reached around her back, unclasping her bra. Her breast bounced from sudden freedom. She laid back down, so he could pull her bra off. He tossed it off the bed and nuzzled her neck. Tony took her breast in his hands, lightly massaging them. Annette closed her eyes and enjoyed the pleasure they gave. Her breath hitched as Bryan's tongue lapped at her. Tony took her nipple into his mouth, gently biting and teasing.

"You two spoil me," she gasped as Bryan sucked her clit into his mouth.

"We intended to spoil you for a long time," Tony told her.

"When do I get to play with you?" She asked with a smile.

Tony smiled and they repositioned themselves on the bed. They slid her to the top of the bed. Excitement thrilled her as she realized what they had in mind. It was a circle of pleasure with Bryan devouring her with his tongue, she'd be sucking on Tony while he pleasured Bryan. She took Tony's hard cock in her mouth, matching Bryan's strokes with her own. This was easily her favorite foreplay position. No one was left out.

"Tonight, I want you to ride me," Bryan spoke from between her legs.

Annette wasn't about to disappoint him. She got up, and he slid himself farther onto the bed. Tony positioned himself between Bryan's legs while she straddled on top of him. Tony wrapped his arms around her, easing her down onto Bryan's cock. She laid her head back on Tony's shoulder as she let Bryan fill her.

"Damn, that feels so good," she moaned when she took his full length in.

"Yes, it does." Bryan agreed and licked his thumb.

He pressed his thumb against her swollen bud. Tony pinched her nipples causing them to harden. Tony kissed her neck, whispering for her to lean forward. She didn't stop her strokes as she slid along Bryan's shaft. She leaned forward bringing her lips to Bryan's. His hands wrapped around her, gripping her hair. She felt Tony behind her when Bryan spread his legs farther apart. Bryan's breath hitched as Tony pushed inside of him. Annette grinned at the sheer pleasure portrayed on Bryan's face. She timed her movements with Tony. He wrapped his arms around her waist, bringing her back up with him. They were in sync with each other as they gave Bryan the ride of his life.

"Ah, fuck!" Bryan's head tilted back.

She could tell he was near his breaking point as his cock swelled inside her. Bryan ran his hands up her legs, bringing his thumb to her clit once more. She wouldn't be able to last if he continued much more.

"That's right, love," Tony whispered in her ear. "Come for us."

Tony bit down on her shoulder, and Bryan's thumb slid over her clit. Her orgasm came bursting through. She screamed out in ecstasy. Bryan's cock pumped inside her as he came. Tony's body shook with his own release inside

Bryan. It was the hottest moment of her life. How could they top this?

Her body collapsed down on Bryan. Tony leaned forward resting his head on her back for a moment. This was a complete moment of bliss and peace. Each one spent to the point of exhaustion.

"Wait here, I'll be right back." Tony climb off the bed, pulling himself from Bryan. Bryan's breath hitched much like hers when one of them pulled out.

"I got to say it again. You're fucking amazing," Bryan said looking into her eyes.

"I have to agree, again," Tony said as he came back in the room with a few wet washcloths.

"I have to say, you two are the amazing ones," Annette countered. "How did I get so lucky?"

"We're the lucky ones, love." Tony gave each of them a washcloth.

"I'm going to take a quick shower," she pulled off Bryan. His breath hitched again and she smiled down at him.

They each took a quick shower. Bryan gave her a t-shirt to wear so she'd stay the night with them. It was easy being in their arms. After Tony rewrapped her hand they laid in bed with her in between them. All the lights were off, but the large balcony let in the bright moonlight.

"You know, I thought after the performance tonight, that you two would take me at the same time. It is something that we haven't done yet."

"When we take you together, we'll be claiming you. You'll be ours, forever." Bryan told her.

"I'm already yours for as long as you'll have me."

"Soon, love." Tony said as they both kissed her temples. "I was thinking maybe you'd like to go for a ride tomorrow?"

"I just went for a ride," she teased.

"I mean on our motorcycles. We try to take a little joy ride out of the city when we have a day off together," Tony explained.

"Braelynn and Ronan get back tomorrow. I'm helping Braelynn pack up her apartment," she said. "It may take all day, but I'd love to go for a ride one day."

"Will we see you tomorrow?" Bryan asked.

"Of course, I'll come by once we're done."

"Deal," Bryan and Tony said in unison.

Annette gave both of them a kiss before closing her eyes. She waited for peaceful sleep but her mind stayed on the men at her sides. She had been falling in love with them from the start. She just hadn't realized it until tonight. For the love of fire and ice, she would do anything for them. Even stand up to a dragon. With that thought, sleep finally took over.

Ten

"I still can't believe Gerri matched you up with Tony and Bryan." Braelynn poured them both a glass of wine. "I bet sex with both of them is incredible."

"Oh, it's amazing," Annette swooned. "I don't know if it's the mind link or what, but they know exactly how I want it."

"We should introduce BJ to Gerri," Braelynn suggested. "She hasn't been on a date since Dave."

"Good luck with that." Annette laughed.

"We'll figure something out." Braelynn shrugged. "What are you going to do about Mara? I don't remember them ever mentioning her."

"I don't know. but I don't want her anywhere near them. There's something off about her."

"Man, I wish I could have been there to see you knock the shit out of her. Talk about a priceless moment."

"Oh, it came with a price." Annette rubbed her wrapped hand. "My knuckles were the price."

"Yeah, but it felt good didn't it?"

"It did make me feel better." Annette laughed. "I think it only fueled the fire though."

"Let me know if you need a partner in crime. We'll kick the bitch's ass together," Braelynn told her.

They laughed together. They hadn't had a girl's day in weeks. Annette put the last of Braelynn's books in a box. That was the last box for the living room. In the past two hours they had only gotten the kitchen and living room packed.

"This is going to take all afternoon," Annette said, looking at the wall of boxes.

"I didn't know I had this much shit." Braelynn laughed. "We'll order pizza in a bit."

"Do you have anymore newspaper? I'll wrap up the hallway knick-knacks."

"Let me check. I think we used it all." Braelynn went into the kitchen. She rummaged around, looking under empty boxes. "Nope, it's all gone. I can get Ronan to bring some by later."

"No worries, I'll run over to my apartment. I have a few in the recycling bin," Annette offered.

"Okay, hurry back." Braelynn opened another empty box.

Annette grabbed her keys from the table by the door. She only lived a few doors down the hall so it wouldn't take long. As she came to her door, she noticed it was ajar. She could've sworn she locked it when she left earlier. Without touching the doorknob, she pushed it open farther to look inside.

"What the hell?" Her apartment had been ransacked.

She didn't hear anyone inside her apartment but she wasn't taking any chances. She left the door open and ran back down the hall to Braelynn's.

"What's the rush?" Braelynn asked when Annette came running in. "Where's the newspaper?"

"I need my phone." Annette ran over to her purse and grabbed her phone. "You're not going to believe this. Someone broke into my apartment."

"What?" Braelynn asked in disbelief.

"You want to come with me?"

"Are you sure that's smart? Maybe you should wait for the police," Braelynn suggested.

"I'm calling them now. I'm still going over there. I just don't want to go alone," Annette admitted. Braelynn closed her eyes. Annette knew she was communicating with Ronan through their bond.

"I told Ronan. He's on his way," Braelynn told her.

As they walked back to Annette's apartment she gave the 911 dispatcher her address. When she got off the phone, she sent a quick text to Bryan and Tony. Not going into details, but letting them know what happened.

"Oh my," Braelynn covered her mouth with her hand when she saw the mess. "Who would've done this?"

"I can only think of one person who would want to do this." Annette said looking at the destruction. "That bitch from last night, Mara."

"How would she know where you live?" Braelynn asked.

"I have no clue," she stepped farther into the living room. "Maybe she followed me, but I didn't leave the building until this morning. I don't see her as being the type that would sit out in a parking garage all night waiting for me to leave. I'm sure she sees her time as too precious."

"Damn, love," Bryan spoke from the doorway.

"How did you get here that fast?" Annette stepped into Bryan's embrace.

"We were down the street at the leather shop picking you up a little something." Tony held up a large bag. He didn't give her the bag, instead he wrapped her up in his arms. "I'm glad you're okay."

"I wasn't here, thankfully." She gave both men a soft kiss. "I'm glad you're here. We were about to do a walk through."

"You should have waited before coming in here." Bryan told her.

"I told Braelynn to wait," Ronan came into Annette's apartment. He gave Braelynn a kiss then shook hands with Bryan and Tony.

"I told her we should wait for the police," Braelynn told Ronan.

"Yeah, I don't listen very well," Annette admitted.

"I remember," Ronan said.

Tony and Bryan led the way down the hall. They checked each room to make sure no one was still in the apartment. Every room had been destroyed. Her bedroom had been the focus point. Everything was broken. Her clothes were ripped up and thrown on the floor. Feathers from her pillow were still blowing around from the wind of her ceiling fan. Even her mattress was ripped, down to the springs.

"I guess this is what happens when you go up against a shifter." Annette forced a laugh. Bryan and Tony wrapped her in their embrace and she buried her head between their chests.

"Annette, being up against a crazy shifter isn't something to laugh about," Braelynn told her.

"You shouldn't stay here," Bryan said. "Why don't you stay with us for a few days?"

"I'll try and pack a bag, if there's anything left." Annette looked around at her shredded clothes. "When I get finished at Braelynn's, I'll come by."

"We can finish another day," Braelynn offered.

"No, it's fine. It'll give me something else to think about besides this mess."

"Suit yourself, I'm not turning down help." Braelynn shrugged.

"Ronan, by any chance did two dragon shifters come through you recently? Maybe in the last few weeks?" Bryan asked.

"As a matter of fact, I did have two Dragos

brothers come from Nova Aurora last month. Why do you ask?" Ronan answered.

"Because we need to find Mara. She's likely responsible for this. Mara said she's staying with them for a while."

"How can you be sure it's the same ones?" Ronan asked.

"Do you get a lot of dragon shifter clients?" Tony asked, raising an eyebrow.

"Their names are Thierno and Amadou," Bryan told Ronan.

"Yeah, it was them," Ronan said as they walked back out into the living room. "But I can't give you their address."

"Seriously?" Tony said as Ronan picked up one of Annette's old bills.

"Like I said, I can't tell you the address," Ronan pulled a pen from his inside jacket pocket. "But if you just happen to come across their address laying around, then that's on you and not me." Ronan scribbled something on the back of the envelope and tossed it on the floor at Bryan's feet.

"Thanks, man." Bryan grabbed the envelope and flipped it over. He folded it and shoved it in his pocket.

"I didn't do anything," Ronan said and turned to Braelynn. "I have to go back to work, beautiful. I'll see you at home later." He kissed Braelynn. "Please be careful."

"It's okay, we won't be here long," Braelynn told him and gave him a hug. Ronan left through the open door.

"The police should be here any minute," Annette commented.

"Good, we're going to find Mara. Keep the door locked until the police show up." Tony said stepping closer to her.

"I will," she kissed him softly. "You two be careful."

"Don't worry about us, love." Bryan stepped in front of her and claimed her lips. "We'll see you later."

She nodded as they walked out of her apartment. Annette closed the door behind them, and locked it. She looked around at the mess and sighed. It would take hours to clean the place up.

"We can't touch anything until after the police come," Annette stopped Braelynn from picking up a broken picture frame.

"Did you see anything missing?" Braelynn asked.

"It's hard to tell. She broke everything." Annette was near tears but managed to hold them back. "How did we not hear any of this? The walls are thin. I have to suffer through Ms. Miller having sex once a week, but she didn't hear anyone smashing my tv?"

"She should have. The old bitty is always home," Braelynn agreed.

"You want to come over for a house cleaning party?" She smiled.

"I'll bring the trash bags, if you can talk Bryan into making a pitcher of that fabulous fruity cocktail." Braelynn bargained. "He'll know the one."

"Deal," Annette agreed. She could go for one of those cocktails right now.

There was a knock at the door and the police announced their arrival. Braelynn went back to her apartment after Annette promised to come over the second the police left. The officer took her statement while an investigation team snapped pictures and dusted for prints. They were all up in her things, putting black dust on anything that would hold a print. She walked through with the officer to see if anything was missing. Nothing appeared to be gone, just broken. Her jewelry had been thrown to the floor, necklaces broken, and rings bent.

"I think anything of value is broken," she told him.

"If you do find something missing, let me know. Make a list of damages and we'll get that logged in with the report. Do you have a place to stay tonight?" He asked.

"Yeah, I'm not staying here." She wouldn't be tackling this mess until tomorrow.

"Good. Herald will need your fingerprints to compare to the prints collected." He told her.

For the Love of Fire and Ice

He left after confirming her contact information, leaving the investigation team to finish with the pictures. An hour later she was alone in her apartment, finally able to touch her stuff. There's not much she would be able to salvage. Hopefully some of her clothes made it unscathed. She went down the hall to her bedroom. The door was closed, and she hadn't shut it. Maybe one of the men on the team closed it behind themselves. She shrugged it off and opened her door. She groaned looking at the disaster in her room. Her bookbag was lying near the dresser, one strap ripped clean off. Is there nothing Mara left untouched? Her dresser drawers were empty. All her clothes were scattered on the floor, most ripped to shreds. She sat down, trying to find something that would cover her body tomorrow. She'd have to buy everything all over again. She did manage to find an old t-shirt and a pair of shorts that survived the attack. Out of the corner of her eyes she spotted her driver's license laying under the door.

"How the hell did you get there?" She crawled over to the door, closing it to pick up her license.

Could it have fallen out of her wallet when her purse fell in the restroom? Who ever trashed her apartment must have been at the club last night. Mara didn't go in the restroom after her because she was escorted out, and she didn't see Mara in the restroom with her. Could it have been someone else who just happened to find her license? Annette still firmly believed it was Mara. Any one else would have stolen things, not trashed everything. Annette reached for the door knob to help her up. Her hand landed in something wet. She jerked her hand away.

"What the hell?" She looked at her hand. It was coated in blood.

She grabbed a torn-up shirt and frantically wiped the blood from her hand. She stood up, looking at the door. Strange symbols were drawn in blood forming a circle on the back of her door. Annette had a terrible feeling about this. How could the police have missed this? The blood was still wet, it couldn't have been put here too long ago. Not wanting to stay in her apartment a minute longer, she grabbed her book bag. Using the cut-up shirt, she opened her bedroom door. As she was leaving something wrapped around her neck jerking her back. Her first instinct was to fight back. She kicked her foot behind her, connecting with a shin. Jerking away from her attacker, Annette spun around ready to punch. No one was there. Frantically, she spun around looking for a target but she didn't see anyone. Suddenly a necklace was placed around her neck with a large jewel pendant dangling down.

"Now my pet, stop fighting." Annette heard Mara's voice.

Instantly, her hands went to her sides. She tried to punch out but her hands weren't moving. She tried to kick but her feet stayed firmly planted where she stood.

"What did you do to me?" Annette demanded to know.

"I can do anything with a little of your DNA," Mara grinned. "Your brush provided all that I needed."

"He-lp," Annette screamed.

"Don't scream," Mara ordered.

Annette's throat closed like someone had their hands around her neck.

"See? That's better," Mara said, smoothing Annette's hair down beside her face. "Nice and quiet. It's not like anyone can hear you. There are charms spread out keeping all sound from escaping."

"What do you want?" Annette's voice was barely above a whisper.

"Same thing I wanted yesterday." Mara said. "I want Bryan to come home and I'm going to use you to get him there."

"He won't go back to Nova Aurora," she told Mara.

"He will if you're there. Of course, I could just kill you and make it look like you're n Nova Aurora, but where's the fun in that?"

"I'm not going anywhere with you."

"You will the second I tell you to," Mara stared at her. "What? Don't believe me? Jump on one foot."

Annette's body followed Mara's demand. She hopped on one foot and continued to hop even though her calf muscle ached. Maybe Ms. Miller will hear her and complain about the noise. Sadly, with Mara's charms chances of someone hearing her were slim.

"You can stop, now that I proved my point," Mara said. "We need to get moving."

"I won't help you."

"I don't need your help." Mara laughed. "Move over there by the bed. I need to prepare for our trip."

Annette's legs moved on their own accord, taking three steps over to the bed. Mara turned her back to Annette and closed the bedroom door. Annette tried over and over to move her body. She tried to scream but her throat tightened once more.

She didn't want Mara to get her nasty hands on Bryan. Not wanting Bryan or Tony to fall for

Mara's trap, she tried to block the mental link between them. Even though she didn't have the faintest idea how to do that. It was important they didn't come. If they knew what was happening, she knew they would follow in a heartbeat. What would Mara do if Bryan didn't come? She was willing to take whatever the risk if it meant she could keep them safe.

"Come here," Mara pulled a strange looking knife from her waistband. "Hold out your hand."

Annette's body obeyed Mara. She walked up next to Mara holding out her unwrapped hand. Mara raised the knife and sliced down Annette's open palm.

"Shit, what the hell was that for?" Annette hissed.

She wanted to close her hand and pull it back to her, but it stayed open. Mara caught the dripping blood on the blade of the knife. She dipped her finger in Annette's blood and turned back to the closed door. She drew another symbol in the middle of the circle. Mara chanted in a language Annette couldn't understand.

Light pierced through the center of the door, circling around it and creating an opening. Annette's eyes widened with shock. Her bedroom door was no longer there. In its place was a doorway size portal made of dark swirls and bright lights.

"This will be fun, for me not you. Who knows, maybe the trip will drain all your weak human life force." Mara shrugged. "It doesn't really matter though. I'll still have control over your body. You'll still serve your purpose, dead or alive."

"You're one evil bitch, you know that?" Annette gritted out.

"Thank you," Mara looked her over. "Wrap your hand. I don't want you bleeding all over my place."

Annette couldn't help but do as she was told. She wrapped her hand in one of the ripped shirts lying on the floor.

"Come on," Mara grabbed her arm and pulled her into the portal.

Annette tried to scream but was sucked into the portal before her throat even had the chance to tighten. She was plunged into darkness. A bright light would flash by her but she couldn't pinpoint it. She felt her body being pulled and her eyelids grew heavy. When she woke she was laying on the ground in a wooded area. Her head was pounding.

"Damn, you did make it." Mara sounded disappointed. "Get up, it's time to go."

Annette's body moved no matter how hard she fought it. She felt tired and weak but her body kept pace with Mara. As they walked away from the portal, Annette glanced back.

"Won't the portal close?" Annette worried that Bryan and Tony may follow through it.

"Why would I close it?" Mara laughed. "Leaving it open will lead Bryan straight to me. Don't worry about your human friend. Only Bryan can come through the portal."

That's what Annette was afraid of. They came to a cliff, just past the trees. It was steep and Annette didn't see a path to follow.

"Halfway up this cliff is a cave. It has a large entrance. You can't miss it."

"You want me to climb that cliff?" Annette asked in disbelief, looking up at the cliff. "I'll never make it."

"Your body will, and that's all I need." Mara shrugged. "Now climb."

Annette moved to the cliff. She didn't even know where would be a good place to start, but her body led the way. As she began to climb, she looked back down at Mara. She had changed into a long-bodied creature. Annette couldn't tell if she was a dragon or a giant lizard. Mara didn't have any wings like the dragon emblems at the penthouse. Mara climbed the cliff effortlessly. Annette watched as Mara entered the cave. She still had a long way to go. Blisters were already forming on her hands. She felt her knee scrape the rock and hissed out in pain as her body forced her higher.

Eleven

"Why would Mara destroy Annette's place?" Bryan asked but didn't really expect Tony to answer.

"Are you serious? Did you see her last night? She was furious," Tony replied. "I bet she would have trashed our place, too, if she were able to get in."

"She's up to something. I know it," Bryan said. "Mara doesn't do anything unless she has a plan."

"Yeah, her plan was to destroy everything Annette has," Tony grumbled.

"She still has us," Bryan pointed out.

"You damn right, she does," Tony agreed. "Turn here."

"Remind me to get Ronan a bottle of our best scotch," Bryan said as they pulled into the long driveway that led to the brother's estate.

"Someone's home." Tony pointed to the car sitting in the circle driveway.

Bryan parked behind the car. They kept an eye out for Mara as they walked up to the front of the house. Bryan pressed the doorbell. Loud chimes sounded on the inside. One thing's for sure, everyone in the house knew someone was at the door. Bryan was determined not to leave until he had some answers out of Mara. One of her brothers answered the door. His expression changed when he saw Bryan.

"What has she done?" Thierno asked.

"Plenty," Bryan replied. "Where is she?"

"Not here," Thierno said. "Come in, I don't know what she's done, but I promise you we had no part in it."

They went inside, and followed Thierno to the den. Amadou stood as they walked in.

"Mara did something, didn't she?" Amadou asked, shaking their hands.

"Were you at the club last night?" Bryan asked.

"Mara came by yesterday. She wanted to go out to dinner and talk. We took her to your restaurant. It's the best in the city," Amadou complimented.

"Thanks," Bryan and Tony said in unison.

"She promised she would stay with us. We were stupid enough to believe she'd stand by her word," Amadou said.

"She's not the same. She's been dealing with dark magic. Has been since you left. We didn't realize her obsession with you had only grown," Thierno informed them.

"Somehow, while we were at dinner, she managed to steal my membership card. I was about to corner her in the restroom. When I went in there, she wasn't there." Amadou told them.

"Maybe you saw the wrong person slip into the restroom," Bryan suggested.

"You don't understand, Bryan." Amadou sat up straight and looked at him. "I know it was her going into that restroom. Yet, no one was in there when I checked. Someone went in but there was no one there. No one came out between her and me."

"We think she's using some type of magic to either transport herself or go invisible," Thierno theorized.

"We need to get back to Annette's. She doesn't leave our sight until Mara is found," Bryan told Tony.

"You didn't tell us what she did," Thierno said, holding out his hand.

"We ran into Mara last night and our girlfriend ended up hitting her," Tony started.

"She hit Mara?" Amadou asked in disbelief. "That's not good. Don't leave her alone with Annette."

"We don't plan on it. Mara was escorted out last night. Today, Annette's apartment was broken into and torn apart. Mara said she was staying here with you." Bryan looked at the brothers.

"Hell no! That's what she wanted at dinner.

We told her she couldn't stay with us. We don't want to deal with that level of crazy. I thought that was why she stole my membership card," Amadou admitted.

"Sorry Mara is causing all this trouble. We'll let you know if she comes back here." Thierno shook their hands.

"Oh, Bryan!" Amadou called out. "She still has my card. Might want to cancel that membership."

"Consider it terminated." Bryan walked out with Tony.

They were silent walking back to the car. Bryan wanted to get back to Annette fast. If Mara was invisible there was no way for Annette to tell that she was there.

"Call Annette." Bryan got in the driver's seat. "See if she made it back to Braelynn's."

Tony took out his phone as Bryan pulled away. Bryan tried to open a link between him and Annette, but there was nothing there.

"Anything?" He asked Tony even though he already knew the answer.

"Nothing," Tony replied. "Each time it goes to voicemail and I can't leave a message. Remind me to get that woman to delete some messages. I have a bad feeling about this, Bryan."

Bryan pressed his foot on the gas, ignoring the speed limits. They made it back to the city in record time. It still wasn't fast enough for him.

"I don't have a link with her," Tony said. "You don't think she learned to block us, do you?"

"Why would she block us?" Bryan asked. "More likely Mara is stopping her somehow. It would take a lot of mental strength to block us without the power of the claiming."

"She's surprised us more than once," Tony reminded him.

"Then I hope that's what it is," Bryan admitted.

He didn't see any police cars when he pulled into the parking garage of the apartments. He had hoped they would still be there. They didn't waste any time after he parked. They ran inside to the elevator. Tony impatiently pressed the button until the elevator doors slid open. The ride seemed slower than it was just hours before. When the doors opened they rushed down the hallway to Annette's door. Tony tried opening the door but it was locked. Bryan knocked on the door. When no one answered he knocked louder.

"Braelynn's apartment is a few doors down." Tony nodded down the hall. "Maybe she already went back over there."

Passing the third door down, they heard a loud thud followed by Braelynn cursing up a storm. Bryan knocked on the door, and the cursing stopped.

"About time," the door swung open. "You're not Annette."

"She hasn't made it back yet?" Bryan asked.

"No, she was going to come back over when the police left," Braelynn told them. "I'll get my keys."

While they waited for Braelynn, they went back to Annette's and knocked on the door again.

"Something's wrong," Tony looked at him. "I can't feel the link."

"When was the last time you linked with her?" Bryan asked not wanting to admit he had the same feeling.

"She was giving the officer her statement, you?" Tony asked in return.

"She was in the middle of having her fingerprints taken."

Braelynn rushed over with her keys. With shaky hands she unlocked the door. Bryan could tell she was nervous and scared for Annette. She could barely get her key in the deadbolt.

"Braelynn, stay out here," Tony told her.

"Not a chance," she starred daggers at him.

"Fine, let us go first then," Bryan offered.

Braelynn nodded and unlocked the deadbolt. All three rushed into the living room. It was still the same mess from earlier.

"Annette!" Bryan and Tony called out.

At a quick glance, Bryan knew Annette wasn't in the living room or the kitchen. They started down the hall, but instantly came to a stop when they saw Annette's bedroom door.

"Forcefield or portal?" Tony asked, taking a few steps closer.

"Judging by the lights, I'm going with portal." Bryan said, then it hit him. "She took Annette to Nova Aurora."

"We have to go after her," Tony told him. "You know it's probably a trap, right?"

"I'm aware, but we have to get Annette back."

"You need to be careful," Tony kissed him like his life depended on it. "Whatever Mara has planned will be aimed at you."

"I want to go," Braelynn said, peering over their shoulders.

"Braelynn, look at me." Bryan turned her to face him. "We know nothing of this portal or how it was made. Portals are dangerous and they don't just pop up with a snap of your fingers. This involved magic. You could be ripped to shreds like Annette's clothes. There's no way to know for sure. Do not go into this portal. If the portal closes let Ronan know. We may need help getting her back."

"I'll keep a look out then. Ronan's on his way, too."

"Good, we'll bring Annette back," Bryan assured her.

"Good luck." Braelynn gave them quick hugs.

Bryan wrapped his arms around Tony, giving him one last kiss. They both took a deep breath and stepped into the portal. Instantly, they were pulled deeper into darkness.

Twelve

Annette finally reached the ledge of the cave. Her leg swung over the ledge and her body rolled itself onto the solid floor of the cave. She was exhausted, her body ached, and her hands burned. The t-shirt bandage was already soaked with blood from the cut on her palm. Blood dripped down her leg from her scrapped knee.

"I was kind of hoping you'd fall," Mara walked over to her with her arms crossed. Her displeasure showing.

"Sorry to disappoint you," Annette's voice cracked. Her throat parched from the climb.

"I won't be disappointed. Come along," Mara snapped her fingers.

Annette's body moved even though all she

wanted to do was rest. She followed Mara into the opening of the cave. She was surprised to find that the cave was Mara's home. Deep inside, it didn't resemble a cave other than the stone wall and ceiling. Pictures hung on the wall of Mara and Bryan from years ago. Even in the photos, Annette could tell Bryan wasn't happy. His smile seemed forced, almost painful. Was he ever happy in his relationship with Mara? From the part of Mara that Annette had seen, she didn't see how anyone could be happy with her unless they were evil themselves.

"You see that rug over there?" Mara pointed to a large area rug in the corner of the main room. "I want you to stand in the center."

"Why?" Annette asked, but her body followed Mara's instructions.

Mara didn't respond, only grinned. She felt a static pulse as she stepped onto the rug. She didn't have to be part of this world to know she stepped through something magical. When she was in the center she turned to face Mara. Annette wanted to smack that grin off her face.

Mara looked up at the ceiling and clapped her hands. A large metal cage came crashing down around Annette where she felt the static.

"Why the cage? You already have power over my body?"

"You think that's for you?" Mara laughed. "Please, you're in no shape to kill a fly. You're helpless. The only reason you're still standing is because I have control. Wanna know how you really feel?" Mara's grin widened into a devilish smile.

Mara snapped her fingers. The weight of the journey slammed into her. Her legs instantly gave out. She collapsed to the rug. Her body hurt bad enough to bring tears to her eyes but she wasn't going to give Mara the satisfaction of seeing her cry. Her body felt heavy. She tried to move her hand but the muscles in her arm protested.

"See? Helpless." Mara ran one of her pointy fingers down a bar of the cage. "I don't need a cage for you. This beauty is for Bryan. He will come for you. Only his love for you will get him through that portal. He'll see you hurt and helpless, like the pathetic damsel in distress you are. He'll rush to your side, getting trapped in this wonderfully crafted fire-resistant cage. It was specially designed for him and his dragon."

"He won't fall for that," Annette made slight movements with her arm. If she could inch her hand to her chest, she could rip the necklace off and be free of Mara's hold.

"Nice try," Mara noticed her movements.

Annette went to snatch the necklace off but Mara was quicker as she snapped her fingers. Annette's body stiffened. Mara had control once more.

"Lay back down and listen," Mara spoke and Annette had no choice but to obey. "Don't speak to anyone. The next person to step on this rug…kill him."

Annette's eyes widened. No way was she going to do this. She had to get the necklace off. She had to warn them not to come. She tried to link with them by calling out in her mind. Annette was so weak that she could barely hold her eyes open. Mara pulled out the knife she used on Annette's hand. She tossed the knife in front of Annette. It landed inches from her face. Mara grabbed one of the bars with her hand, chanting her magical spell. The bars on the cage disappeared before Annette's eyes. Mara's hand went straight through where the bar was moments before.

"Now he can get in, but no one can get out. Slip the knife underneath you, and lay back down. He can just walk in none the wiser to the cage. Use the knife when he leans down to check on you. Either you kill him, or die trying." Mara shrugged her shoulders.

Annette would rather die than cause harm to Bryan or Tony. She tried again to make a connection with them. She closed her eyes and repeated their names in her mind. When she blocked them earlier, maybe she broke the connection. What if she couldn't connect with them anymore? It didn't matter, she still had to try.

"Our guest should be here soon. I'll be back,"

Mara warned.

Mara walked deeper into the cave, leaving Annette alone with her thoughts. She tried with all her might to break free, but the control Mara had was too strong. Anger stirred inside Annette. If she ever got out of this, she was going to plunge that knife into Mara's black heart.

Loud thuds sounded outside the cave. The cave floor shook below her. It had to be them. Annette wanted to run to them, and get as far away from this cave as possible. She tried to move her legs, but it was still no use. A tear slid down her cheek, knowing what was to come.

From where she laid, she couldn't see who came in. She was surprised when she saw Tony come around the end of the couch. She screamed in her head for him to stop. She tried to speak, her throat closed up so fast she thought she'd black out. Mara was using her as a puppet and there was nothing she could do about it. She pleaded with her eyes for him to stop. He only picked up his pace as Bryan came near. Tony stepped on the rug, pausing a step in.

"Bryan, stay away. There's something here," Tony warned.

"No!" Mara screamed from the depths of the cage. "You're not supposed to be here."

"I've got Mara, you take care of Annette." Bryan ran out of Annette's sight, following where Mara voice had come from.

"Annette, love. What has she done to you?" Tony bent down next to her. A tear fell as her hands tightened on the knife hilt.

I'm sorry, she said in her head as her hand came out from under her. Tony was quick enough to hit her hand out of the way. The blade nicked his skin. Her body moved on its own, bringing the knife around for another swing. Tony blocked her again and grabbed her wrist, temporarily stopping her attack.

"Love, you've been bewitched. Put down the knife," Tony spoke calmly.

Her knee came up connecting with his inner thigh. He grunted and wrapped his arm around her leg, lifting her off the ground. Her back hit the bars and suddenly they were visible again. Tony looked at the cage around them. Her free hand fisted and connected with his face.

"Love, I thought you didn't like torture chambers?" He smiled and kissed her lips.

She wanted nothing more than to kiss him back at this moment. Her fist came down on his back and he bit her lip. *The necklace*, she shouted in her mind. Over and over she repeated it. He had to get the necklace off. It was the only way to get her free will back. Tony pinned her free arm with his shoulder.

"You know, this would be sexy if I didn't think you were trying to kill me." Tony spoke in her ear. "I'm sorry it's come to this."

Tony blew his cold breath on the hilt of the knife. She felt her hand getting colder but she couldn't drop the knife. She tried to scream, but her throat tightened to where no sound came out. Tony must have realized she couldn't drop the knife and stopped his assault.

"Damn it, love. I'm sorry." He brought her cold hand to his lips. "I thought a kiss would break the spell."

The necklace, she pleaded. Her leg tried to kick out but Tony had her pinned with all his weight. He looked her over, his eyes finally coming to rest on the necklace. He let go of her leg. She freed it to kick him in the shin. Tony grabbed a hold of the pendant around her neck and yanked it off. Immediately her body was hers again. The knife dropped from her hands. Her weight was too much for her to hold. She fell into his arms.

"I got you, love," he eased her down to the rug. Her first movement of free will was to bring him to her lips. "Why did you block us?"

"I was trying to protect you," she tried to smile.

"Funny, way of protecting me." Tony looked at the nick in his side.

"I'm sorry. It wasn't me," she began but he cut her off by kissing her.

"I know, love." Tony looked around at the

cage once more. "I need to help Bryan." They could hear Mara's frustrated screams down the hall.

"She can disappear," she warned Tony.

"Yeah, we found out from her brothers," he informed her.

"We can't get out of the cage. Mara said it was designed specially for Bryan."

"Designed for Bryan not me. It was made to hold a fire dragon." Tony went to the bars. "I can break these."

"How?"

"By freezing them then using my dragon to bust through," he told her with a smile.

"You're going to turn into a dragon, in here?" She asked worried she'll get squashed in the process.

"Once I freeze the bars, I need you to stand in the corner. Make yourself as small as possible," he instructed.

Tony blew cold air onto the bars. Annette feared it wouldn't work until she heard the bars start to freeze over. He took a few deep breaths and blew again. This time, the bars glassed over with ice until the bars themselves turned a shade of blue. Annette crouched down in the corner next to the cold bars, trying to make herself as small as possible. Tony smiled over at her as his transformation began. His face elongated, and his body swelled. His clothes were replaced with large scaled skin. His long tail wrapped around his body to fit in the cage. His scales were a deep blue with white spiked horns running along his face. He arched his body up, pressing against the frozen bars. All at once he pushed and swung his tail out. Bars flew out across the room as they broke from the cage.

"Incredible!" Annette jumped up. The movement was a little too fast for her body and she became light headed.

"Easy, love," Tony's dragon said in a deep voice. "Get on, I don't want you out of my sight while she's loose."

Annette picked up the knife, Mara wanted her to kill with. Without the necklace there was nothing stopping her from whooping Mara's ass now. She put the knife in the waistband of her shorts and climbed on Tony's back. His scales felt strange on her legs but it wasn't a bad strange.

"I'm ready," she told him.

Together they went in search of Bryan and Mara. The cave was deeper and larger than Annette thought. Tony was easily able to fit down the stone hallway in dragon form. The cave broke off into different tunnels. She felt heat coming from the tunnel on the right of the cave.

"This one goes to the other side of the cliffs." Tony told her in the dragon's deep voice.

A flame shot out towards them from the long hall like tunnel. Annette tucked herself behind Tony. He blew cold air blocking the flames from hitting them. At least they knew they were going in the right direction. The cave opened up into a rear entrance. Mara's laugh came from the left. Bryan's dark red dragon blew flames where her laugh came from, only for Mara to start laughing from the right.

"She's invisible," Annette stated the obvious.

They watched as Mara continued to play cat and mouse with Bryan. They needed a way to see her. Looking around all Annette had was a knife, fire and ice. Thinking for a few seconds, she came up with an idea. She patted Tony's long neck to get his attention. When he turned his head toward her. She whispered in his ear. He'll be able to communicate the plan with Bryan. Mara laughed moving around the room. An electric orb flew toward Bryan's dragon, hitting him on his left wing. Annette wanted to run to him, but Tony backed up. He turned around and spread his wings out creating a barrier between her and Mara. Tony breathed out, blowing a blue liquid. It crackled and turned to icicles on the ceiling. The more he blew the longer and wider the icicles became until they reached the floor trapping Mara in with them. Tony carried her back to the opening where Mara and Bryan were still fighting. With long breaths Tony covered the cave floor and walls with a thin coat of ice.

They heard Mara scream out from the right as she slipped on the ice. A clay pot busted by the right wall. Bryan blew a flame towards the broken pot, catching Mara's arm with the flame. Her arm charred for only a second then disappeared like the rest of her. Annette was done feeling helpless. She wiggled herself higher on Tony's neck, trying to see over him. *I'm not helpless*, she told herself. She pulled the knife from her waistband. She didn't win dart tournaments three years in a row for nothing. Patiently she waited for the ice to crack. Suddenly it cracked in the center of the room. Bryan shot out a flame hitting her leg. That was all the target Annette needed. Before the char marks disappeared, Annette threw the knife a couple of feet higher. Mara screamed as the knife appeared to be floating in mid-air. Bryan didn't throw another flame at Mara as she fell to the ice. The ice turned red, coated with Mara's blood. Her body slowly started to appear again. She clenched the knife at her chest and stared at Annette. She saw nothing but pure hatred in Mara's eyes.

"I'm not that helpless after all, am I?" Annette said to Mara.

Bryan warmed the floor, melting the ice so Annette could get down. She climbed off Tony as Bryan shifted back to his human form. Annette ran up to him jumping in his arms. She kissed him long and hard. Tony came up behind them, engulfing them both in a tight hug.

"I'm glad we're together again," she told them. She kissed them both in turn.

"Where did you learn to throw a knife?" Bryan asked her, looking back down to Mara.

"I don't know how to throw a knife. I can hit a bullseye with a dart every time, though." Annette shrugged. "I figured it couldn't be too much different."

"That was brilliant." Tony kissed her cheek.

"Never block us again," Bryan ordered.

"Deal," Annette agreed. "Can we go home now?

"Of course, love." Tony kissed her cheek.

"I don't have to climb back down the cliff, do I?" Annette asked.

"You climbed all the way up here?" Bryan looked at her in disbelief.

"Afraid so," Annette held up her bloody hands.

"We'll fly you out," Bryan said, then stepped back and shifted into his beautiful red dragon.

Tony helped her onto Bryan's back. Once she was settled, he took a couple of steps back and shifted. She was going home. Not to her torn up apartment but home with Bryan and Tony. There was no other place she'd rather be.

Thirteen

Flying out the cave, Annette finally got the chance to look around at the beautiful scenery of Nova Aurora. The planet was thriving. Everything had a purple hue. They flew over the trees. The different shades of purple was stunning. She held on tight not trusting her muscles. They made distance between them and the cliff fast. Annette looked back, at where she had just taken another's life. The yellowish mountainside stood out from the purple forest.

"What about Mara? Are we just going to leave her there?" She asked loudly so Bryan would hear her.

"Yes," he said simply. His voice deeper than his normal tone.

"We have to hurry back to the portal," Tony flew up next to them. "When she dies, her magic will too. That includes the portal."

"Shit," maybe she shouldn't have gone for the bullseye. No, Annette shook her head. She was right to do what she did. She did it for her loves.

Bryan angled down into the trees. Annette squealed and held on tight as he dodged branches. The portal came into view and it was getting smaller. As Bryan landed, she jumped from his back for him to shift. Tony shifted in mid-land.

"Hurry," they said in unison. Each took one of her battered hands, helping her keep up.

Holding on to each other, they ducked down and ran into the portal. Just as before she was pulled into darkness, but she felt Bryan and Tony with her. She held them as tight as her abused muscles could hold. The longer they were in the darkness, the more drained she felt. She didn't have the magic of the necklace keeping her together this time. Tony and Bryan wrapped their arms around her, incasing her with their bodies. Her eyes closed with extreme exhaustion.

When she awoke, she was laying in Bryan's arms. They were back in her apartment. Her body felt heavy and weak. Bryan's body gave off a welcoming warmth that soothed her aches.

"Welcome back, love." Bryan smiled down at her. He gently pressed a kiss to her lips.

"Told you she was tough," Tony said, leaning down and planting a kiss on her forehead.

"Oh, I'm glad you're up." Braelynn rushed over to her. "When y'all didn't come back, I was beginning to panic."

"I was only gone a couple of hours," Annette told her.

"Annette, you've been gone all night." Braelynn pulled out her phone and showed her the time. "It's three o'clock in the morning."

"Time is a little different on Nova Aurora," Bryan informed them. "We've lived here for six years, but to Mara I was only gone around seven months."

"How did she get to you? I didn't hear a thing." Braelynn helped her stand up and gave her a hug.

Her legs were wobbly and felt worse than running back to back marathons. She decided she'd rather not go through another portal for a long time. She gave them the run down on how Mara swiped her. Not one of her glorious moments that's for sure.

"One thing I don't understand?" Annette turned to Bryan and Tony. "Mara said that Tony couldn't get through the portal. Only Bryan's love for me could bring him through."

"She didn't take into account that I would love you too." Tony wrapped his arms around her. "Our love for you brought us to you."

"Together we can conquer anything," she pressed her lips against his.

Stepping from his embrace, she walked down the hall and saw what was left of her bedroom door. It was still connected to the frame. A large crack formed in a spiderweb like pattern from the center of her door.

"I need to conquer this mess. I don't think I will be getting the security deposit back."

"We can handle this mess another day," Bryan told her. "Right now, you need to relax and let us pamper you."

"I could definitely go for some pampering." She agreed, turning away from her bedroom.

Annette didn't bother to get the bag she had tried to pack. Everything was ruined. She'd start all over tomorrow. Tonight, she just wanted to go home with her men. They were all she needed. She could replace everything else. All that mattered was that they're all safe now.

Annette hugged Braelynn again before she left to go to her apartment with Ronan. Bryan made a call to Mara's brothers. Annette hated that Bryan had to make that call. Even more so that she caused it. She wouldn't blame them if they hated her without having ever met her.

Annette grabbed her purse Braelynn brought over and left her apartment. She locked the door even though there was nothing left to steal that wasn't broken. Tony helped her to the elevator with Bryan in tow. Bryan got off the phone as they stepped on to the elevator.

"How'd it go?" She asked as Bryan put his phone away.

"They knew it was coming. She's one of the reason's they left Nova Aurora after their father died. She's turned on everyone until she had no one left."

"I hope she can find peace wherever she goes from there," Annette admitted.

They led the way to where they parked the car. Her body protested with every step. Tony scooped her up in his arms to carry her the rest of the way to the car. She leaned against him, resting her head on his shoulder. Bryan opened the passenger door and Tony gently set her down in the seat. When Tony got in the back seat he moved the bag he teased her with earlier.

"Do I get what's in the bag yet?" Annette pointed at the bag. Tony looked at Bryan when he got in the driver's seat.

"I think she deserves it," Bryan nodded.

Tony handed her the bag. Like a child on Christmas, she felt giddy for the gift. Opening the bag, she pulled out a large sweater box. It weighed too much to be a new blouse. She set the bag on the floorboard and placed the box in her lap. The smell of new leather hit her the moment she opened the box. She moved the tissue paper out of the way to reveal a beautiful black leather jacket.

"Yay, I now own something that's not cut up." She lifted it from the box.

"Flip it around," Tony said eagerly. She flipped it to the back.

"That's amazing!" Two dragons were embossed in the center, resembling their dragon emblems joined together. "It's beautiful. I love it. If I wasn't so dirty I'd put it on."

"We were going to give it to you when you went on a ride with us." Tony said from behind her.

"I'm glad I got it now," Annette folded it up and closed it back in the box.

"We thought about taking you shopping tomorrow. It's kind of my fault that your stuff got messed up in the first place," Bryan offered.

"Oh no, I couldn't accept that. I wouldn't mind some help cleaning up the mess. I'll have to get rid of some furniture and could use your muscles." She laid her head back against the seat.

"We'll help you with anything you need. We always will," Tony told her.

******

They didn't lie when they said they would pamper her. Tony insisted on carrying her up to the penthouse. She was too sore to protest. He set her down on the bathroom counter while Bryan drew her a hot bath. Tony dipped his finger into the steaming water and shook his head. He blew lightly on top of the water, cooling it down to a comfortable hot instead of pipping hot.

The hot water did wonders for her aching muscles. She'd never been that sore in her life.

While she soaked, Tony and Bryan took showers. They were out of the showers before she was ready to be done. Bryan insisted that she stay in the tub and relax. She had no problem following his request especially when he warmed the water back up for her. Tony patched up Bryan's shoulder where he had gotten hit in the wing. When they left the bathroom, they took her clothes with them to throw in the washer. At least she would have something to wear tomorrow. After she soaked long enough, she washed up. As she was getting out, Tony came into the bathroom with a towel draped over his arm.

"Bryan warmed a towel for you." He held it out for her as she stepped from the tub.

"That was thoughtful." She let him wrap her up in the towel.

"Come sit here." He pointed to the spot next to the sink. "I'll wrap your hands properly."

He picked her up and placed her on the edge of the counter. She held out her cut hand for him. The bleeding has almost stopped. He bandaged the cut and wrapped her hand in gauze. Her knuckles on her other hand were still swollen from the night before. Tony tenderly wrapped her swollen hand, giving it a light blow to chill her sore knuckles.

"I am terribly sorry this happened to you." He kissed her bandaged hands.

"It's over with now." She shrugged. There's nothing they could do about the last 24 hours. All they could do is move forward. "You don't have an ex out for revenge too, do you?"

"No." He laughed. He helped her down from the counter top. Together they left the bathroom to find Bryan.

"Are you hungry? We can get some food sent up," Bryan asked from the kitchen where he was mixing something into a coffee mug.

"I'll eat in the morning. Right now, I just want to hold you two," she admitted.

"Before we do, I want you to drink this." Bryan handed her the coffee mug.

"What is it?" The smell wasn't too pleasant. She scrunched her nose and pulled the mug away.

"Smells like shit, but it's great for the body," Bryan told her. "I promise it won't hurt you."

"Oh, I trust you. It's the smell I'm having the trouble with."

"Then don't smell it. Chug it down and the smell will be gone," Tony offered with a grin.

"You'll thank me shortly." Bryan smiled.

Pinching her nose, she lifted the mug to her lips. The warm liquid coated her mouth. She swallowed the drink back as quickly as she could. It took four large gulps to finish his medicinal concoction. The taste wasn't as bad as the smell. Bryan took the mug and placed it on the counter.

"Do you feel it?" Tony asked a moment later.

"Feel what?" She didn't feel any different.

"Maybe it will take a few minutes," Bryan said taking her hand. "Ready for bed?"

"I've been ready for hours," she replied as they went to lay down in their giant bed.

She dropped her towel at the foot of the bed and climbed into the middle, wanting both their arms around her. They smiled at each other and stripped their pajama pants off. Each took a side and climbed in beside her. She pulled them in close and they wrapped their arms around her. There was a moment she thought she would die and never see them again. To have them back in her arms was the greatest feeling in the world. A strange sensation came over her. Her body began to tingle from her stomach. It was like warm butterflies fluttering over her body. The sensation caught her off guard and she giggled.

"Feel it now?" Tony kissed above her breast.

"What is that?" She asked, as the feeling ran along her extremities.

"It's a muscle remedy my grandmother taught me. Your muscles should be good as new shortly. Though, you're knuckles and cuts will have to heal on their own."

"Thank you." Her body didn't feel as stiff or as sore as it was moments before.

"Told you, you'd be thanking me." Bryan laughed.

"I have other ways to thank you." Annette started to sit up, but Bryan stopped her.

"We still mean what Bryan said. We will be pampering you tonight, well what's left of it." Tony insisted. "You lay back and just enjoy us enjoying you."

"We want to claim you as our own tonight." Bryan said looking into her eyes. "We love you, Annette. You are the only one that can complete us."

Annette knew that when a shifter claimed someone, they claimed for life. She also knew that there were no two other people she would rather be with than Bryan and Tony. She could let them claim her now and do a wedding later on. A claiming would be just between them. They both waited for her response with eagerness. She could never deny them. When she nodded, they pulled her close, each kissing her in turn.

They massaged her body and kissed along her skin. She laid there bare for them to enjoy. Laying her head back on the pillow, she closed her eyes taking in the feel of them on her skin. Tony's cool tongue trailed down her body, then Bryan's warm lips would cover the same trail. The sensations sent shivers throughout her body. They each took one of her legs, spreading her legs open for them. Bryan got the first turn between her thighs. His warm tongue pressed against her and she melted into him. Her body yearned for theirs. Tony sucked her nipple into his mouth. Her body arched with pleasure. Bryan ran his tongue down to her ass and back up to her clit. The movement made her core tighten.

"You like ass play, don't you?" Tony smiled claiming her lips before she could answer.

She'd never let a man enter her there. With Tony and Bryan, she felt relaxed. There was nothing she could think of that she wouldn't let them do to her. Her body was theirs to do what they pleased. Bryan pushed a finger inside her and pressed his thumb on her ass. The pleasure left her wanting more. She could feel Bryan's smile against her as she leaned into him.

Bryan pulled away from her, rolling her to her side. They climbed up beside her, Bryan in front of her and Tony behind her. They position themselves between her legs. She brought her leg over Bryan's hip as he pushed inside of her. Tony grabbed some lube from the nightstand. He waited until Bryan was completely in before pressing his lube covered cock against her ass. She didn't think she'd be able to take Tony inside her at the same time as Bryan. Tony applied pressure with every stroke from Bryan. She felt her ass stretch as Tony pushed inside her. It felt impossible until the head of Tony's cock entered her body. The tightness fell away to pleasure as Tony eased inside her.

She moaned as they pushed deeper into her. *This is what it feels like to be complete.* Their slow and steady pace quickened. Her breath rushed out with each thrust. She reached behind her grabbing Tony's ass, bringing him closer to her.

"I love that tight ass," Tony bit down on her shoulder. She rolled her head against his shoulder and Bryan kissed her breast.

"Perfect." Bryan took her nipple into his mouth.

Passion built as sweat beaded down their bodies. Her release came in a massive explosion that had her screaming breathlessly. '*Mine*' they spoke in unison in her mind as they both bit down on her shoulders, prolonging her climax. Their cum filled her as their cocks pumped inside of her. '*Mine,*' she said in her mind. Thankful, she could hear them again. She didn't realize how much she missed them in her head until that moment. They held her tight, their bodies still sensitive from their release.

"I can hear you again," she told them.

"It's meant to be." Bryan kissed her softly.

"How do you feel?" Tony asked slowly pulling out of her.

"Better than a million bucks," she told him.

After getting cleaned up, she reclaimed her position in the middle of the bed. They climbed back in the bed beside her, resting their heads on her shoulders. She wrapped her arms around them and kissed their foreheads before falling into a deep sleep. She dreamt of the future she would have with her dragons, carrying on their bloodlines with little dragons of their own. She owed Gerri a million thanks for bringing her together with them. She needed to thank her for the love of fire and ice.

About the Author

Living in South Carolina Roxanne enjoys spending time with her family. Books are her escape from a house full of boys. When nerf wars are at a high, she can escape into her own little corner to create an escape for others.

Currently writing paranormal romance Roxanne has plans of dipping into other genres as well. Come and escape into the unknown.

www.facebook.com/AuthorRoxanneWitherell
www.twitter.com/RoxanneAuthor

Other Books by the Author

More books by Roxanne Witherell

<u>O'Neil Pack Series</u>
Mountainside Resort
Fated Temptation
Missing Mate
Remember Mate

<u>Paranormal Dating Agency</u>
Winged Solution

Paranormal Dating Agency World

Thank you for reading my contribution to the PDA World!

Reviews are greatly appreciated.

For more amazing stories in the PDA World follow us on Social Media:

MT World Press website:

http://mtworldspress.com/

MT Shared Worlds Reader Group:

https://www.facebook.com/groups/412969162428913/

MT Worlds Facebook page:

https://www.facebook.com/AlphaPNR/

email: mtwpress1@gmail.com

Made in the USA
Columbia, SC
17 February 2019